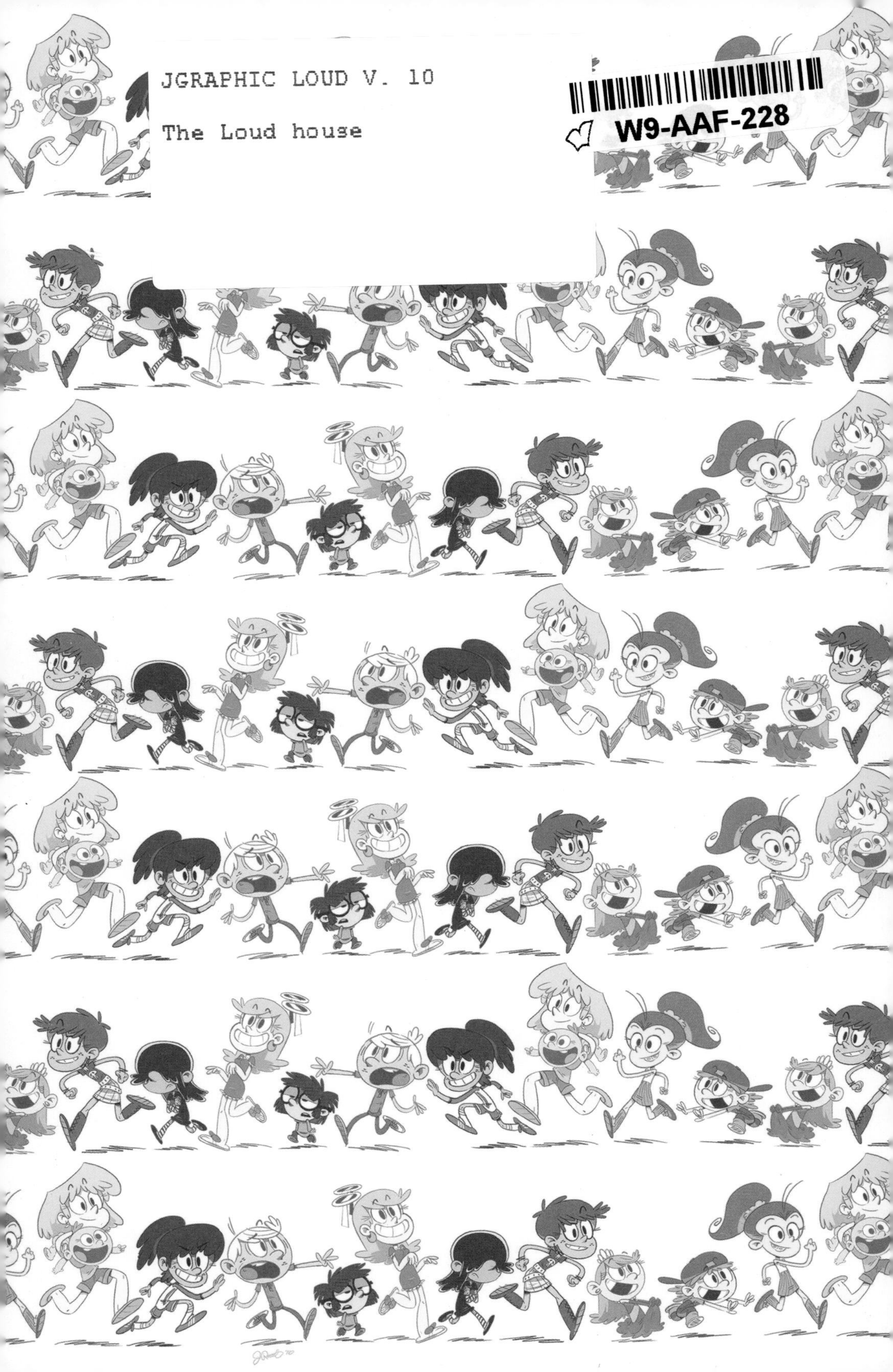

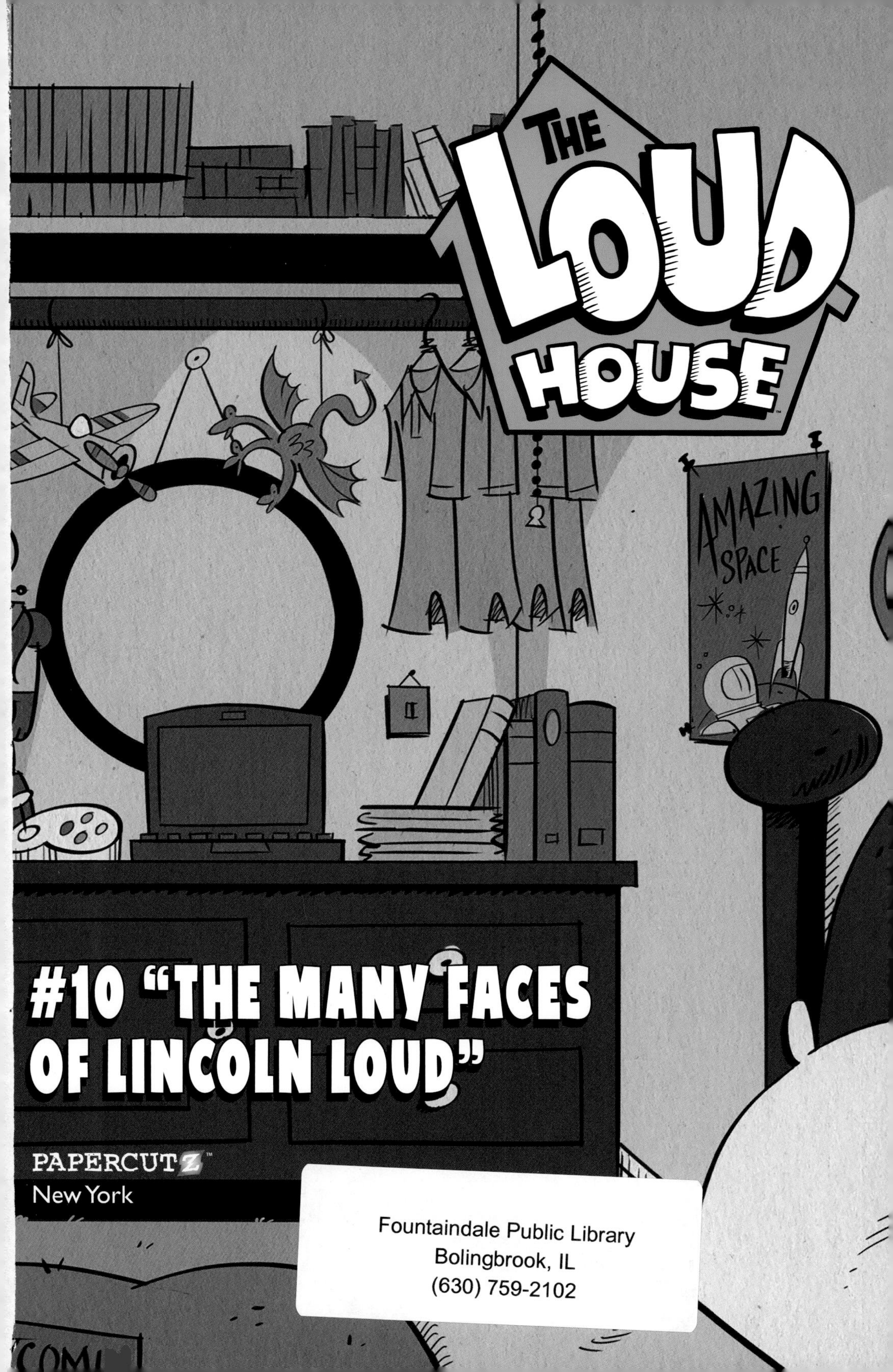
AMAZING SPACE

# THE LOUD HOUSE

## #10 "THE MANY FACES OF LINCOLN LOUD"

PAPERCUTZ™
New York

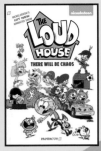

THE LOUD HOUSE
THERE WILL BE CHAOS
PAPERCUTZ
THE LOUD HOUSE
#1
"There Will Be Chaos"

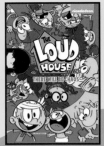

THE LOUD HOUSE
THERE WILL BE CHAOS
THE LOUD HOUSE
#2
"There Will Be More Chaos"

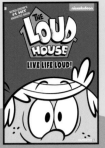

THE LOUD HOUSE
LIVE LIFE LOUD!
THE LOUD HOUSE
#3
"Live Life Loud!"

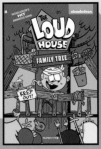

THE LOUD HOUSE
FAMILY TREE
KEEP OUT!
THE LOUD HOUSE
#4
"Family Tree"

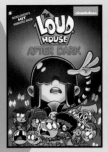

THE LOUD HOUSE
AFTER DARK
THE LOUD HOUSE
#5
"After Dark"

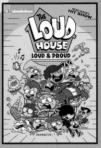

THE LOUD HOUSE
LOUD & PROUD
THE LOUD HOUSE
#6
"Loud and Proud"

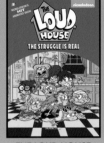

THE LOUD HOUSE
THE STRUGGLE IS REAL
THE LOUD HOUSE
#7
"The Struggle is Real"

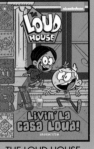

THE LOUD HOUSE
Livin' La Casa Loud!
THE LOUD HOUSE
#8
"Livin' La Casa Loud"

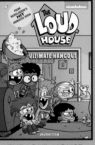

THE LOUD HOUSE
ULTIMATE HANGOUT
THE LOUD HOUSE
#9
"Ultimate Hangout"

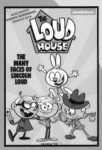

THE LOUD HOUSE
THE MANY FACES OF LINCOLN LOUD
THE LOUD HOUSE
#10
"The Many Faces of Lincoln Loud"

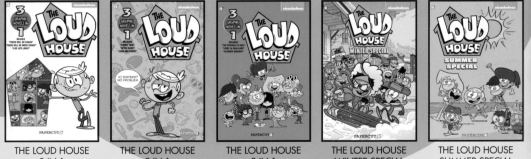

3 GRAPHIC NOVELS IN 1
THE LOUD HOUSE
PAPERCUTZ
THE LOUD HOUSE
3 IN 1
#1

3 GRAPHIC NOVELS IN 1
THE LOUD HOUSE
10 SISTERS? NO PROBLEM.
THE LOUD HOUSE
3 IN 1
#2

3 GRAPHIC NOVELS IN 1
THE LOUD HOUSE
PAPERCUTZ
THE LOUD HOUSE
3 IN 1
#3

COMING SOON

THE LOUD HOUSE
WINTER SPECIAL
PAPERCUTZ
THE LOUD HOUSE
WINTER SPECIAL

COMING SOON

THE LOUD HOUSE
SUMMER SPECIAL
PAPERCUTZ
THE LOUD HOUSE
SUMMER SPECIAL

The Loud House graphic novels are available for $7.99 each in paperback, $12.99 each in hardcover. THE LOUD HOUSE 3 IN 1 graphic novels are available for $14.99 each in paperback only.
Available from booksellers everywhere. You can also order online from Papercutz.com, or call 1-800-886-1223, Monday through Friday, 9-5 EST. MC, Visa, and AmEx accepted. To order by mail, please add $5.00 for postage and handling for the first book ordered, $1.00 for each additional book and make check payable to NBM Publishing.
Send to: Papercutz, 160 Broadway, Suite 700, East Wing, New York, NY 10038.

Nickelo[redacted]ks are sold.

# THE LOUD HOUSE

**#10 "THE MANY FACES OF LINCOLN LOUD"**

nickelodeon™ THE LOUD HOUSE

# #10 "THE MANY FACES OF LINCOLN LOUD"

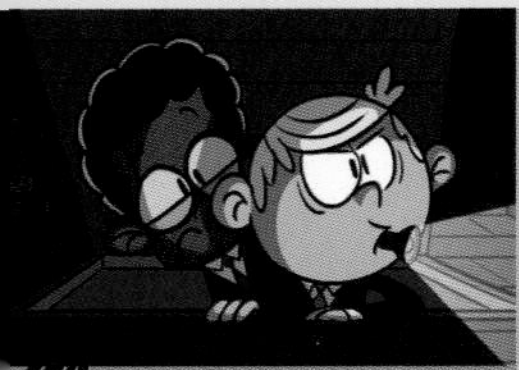

"THE HAUNTED HOUSE"
Derek Fridolfs — Writer
Max Alley — Artist
Amanda Rynda — Colorist
Wilson Ramos Jr. — Letterer

"TWINNING AT LIFE"
Caitlin Fein — Writer
Agny Innocente — Artist, Colorist
Wilson Ramos Jr. — Letterer

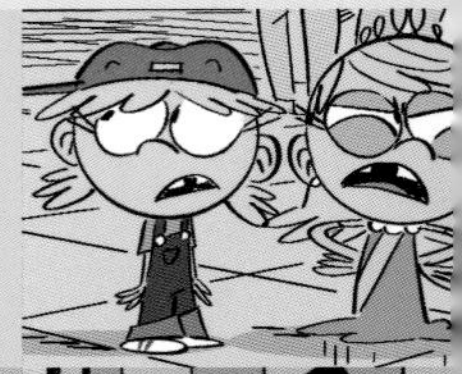

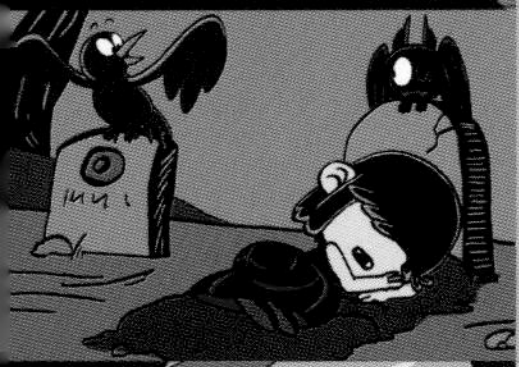

"LUCY OF MELANCHOLIA"
Caitlin Fein — Writer
Gizelle Orbino — Artist, Colorist
Wilson Ramos Jr. — Letterer

"MODEL BEHAVIOR"
Caitlin Fein — Writer
Erin Hyde — Artist, Colorist
Wilson Ramos Jr. — Letterer

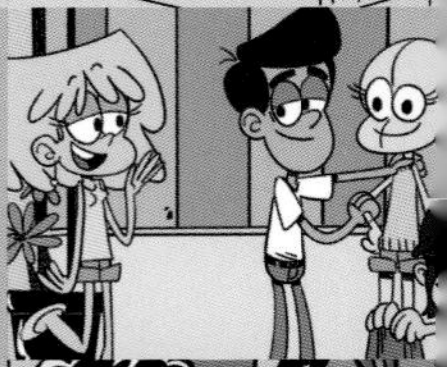

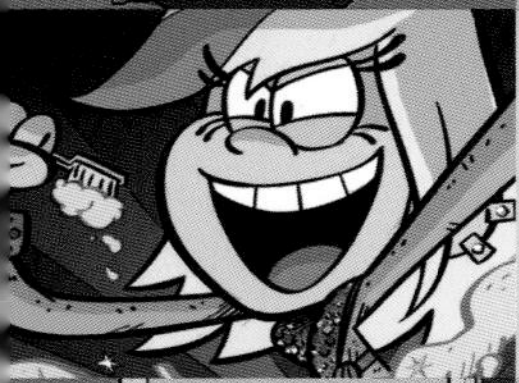

"ROCKIN' ROUTINE"
Kiernan Sjursen-Lien — Writer
Lee-Roy Lahe — Artist
Hallie Lal — Colorist
Wilson Ramos Jr. — Letterer

"TERMS OF ENDEARMENT"
Jared Morgan — Writer, Artist, Colorist, Letterer

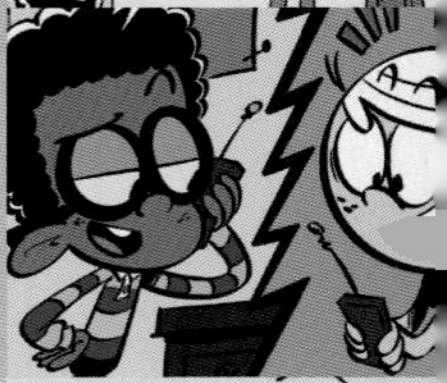

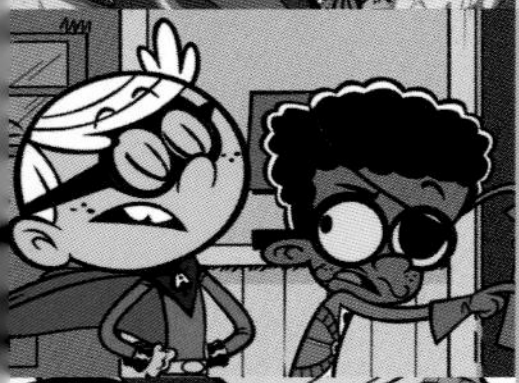

"NONE CHUCKED"
Derek Fridolfs, Zazo Aguiar — Writers
Zazo Aguiar — Artist, Colorist
Wilson Ramos Jr. — Letterer

"BRACE FOR IT"
Derek Fridolfs — Writer
Kelsey Wooley — Artist, Colorist
Wilson Ramos Jr. — Letterer

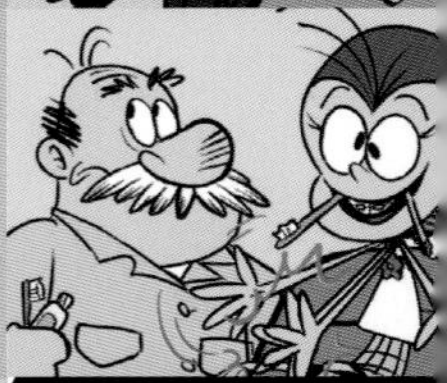

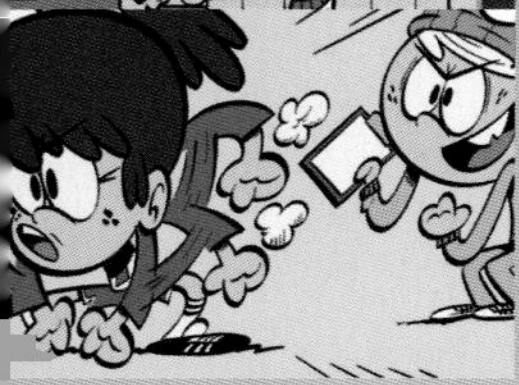

"BIG GAINS"
Jared Morgan — Writer, Artist, Colorist, Letterer

"CANDY HUNTING AT HUNTINGTON MANOR"
Sammie Crowley — Writer
Ari Castleton — Artist
Gabrielle Dolbey — Colorist
Wilson Ramos Jr. — Letterer

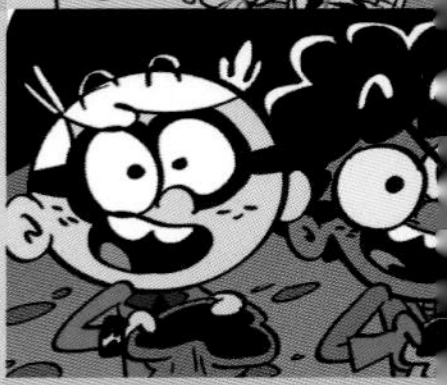

COLTON DAVIS — Cover Artist
JORDAN ROSATO — Endpapers
JAMES SALERNO — Sr. Art Director/Nickelodeon
JAYJAY JACKSON — Design
SAMMIE CROWLEY, SEAN GANTKA, ANGELA ENTZMINGER, DANA CLUVERIUS, MOLLIE FREILICH, ASHLEY KLIMENT, AMANDA RYNDA, SONIA CANO, JARED MORGAN, CAITLIN FEIN — Special Thanks
JEFF WHITMAN — Editor
JOAN HILTY — Editor/Nickelodeon
JIM SALICRUP
Editor-in-Chief

ISBN: 978-1-5458-0473-5 paperback edition
ISBN: 978-1-5458-0474-2 hardcover edition


www.papercutz.com

Papercutz books may be purchased for business or promotional use. For information on bulk purchases please contact Macmillan Corporate and Premium Sales Department at (800) 221-7945 x5442.

Printed in China
August 2020

Distributed by Macmillan
First Printing

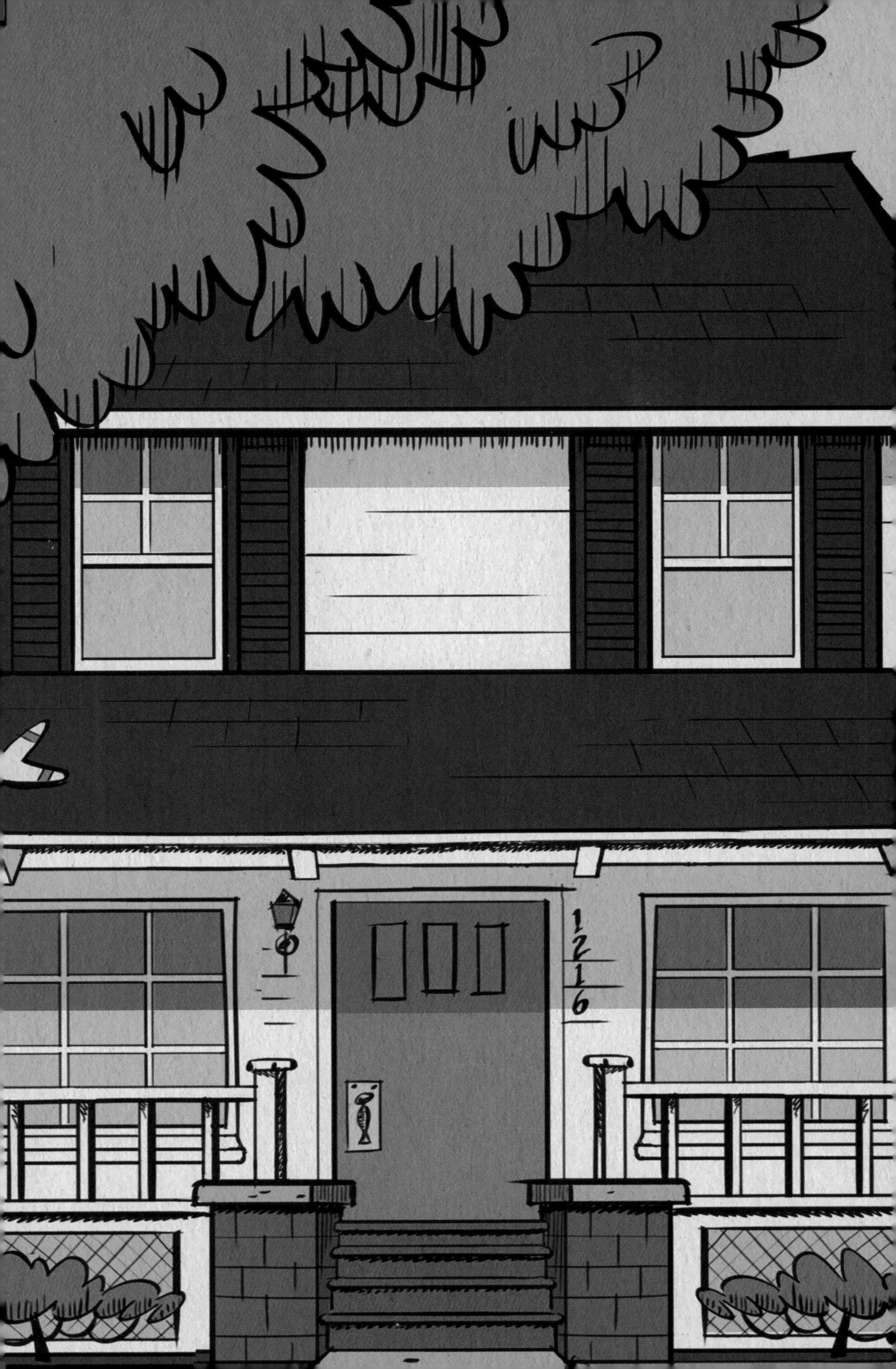
1216

# MEET THE LOUD FAMILY *and friends!*

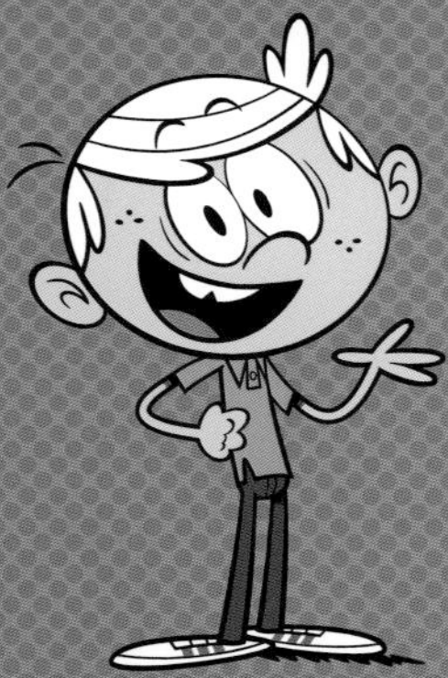

## LINCOLN LOUD
THE MIDDLE CHILD (11)

At 11 years old, Lincoln is the middle child, with five older sisters and five younger sisters. He has learned that surviving the Loud household means staying a step ahead. He's the man with a plan, always coming up with a way to get what he wants or deal with a problem, even if things inevitably go wrong. Being the only boy comes with some perks. Lincoln gets his own room – even if it's just a converted linen closet. On the other hand, being the only boy also means he sometimes gets a little too much attention from his sisters. They mother him, tease him, and use him as the occasional lab rat or fashion show participant. Lincoln's sisters may drive him crazy, but he loves them and is always willing to help out if they need him.

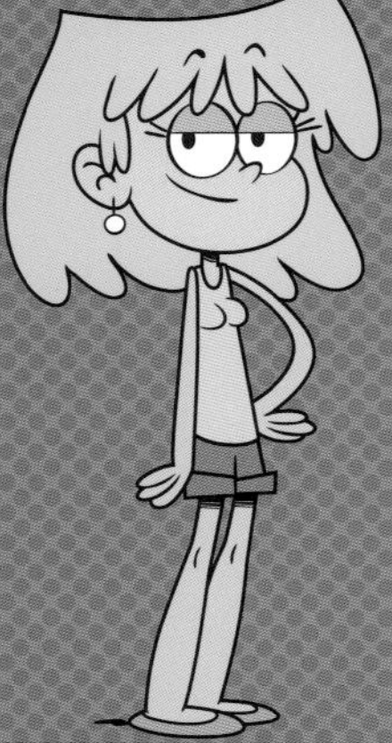

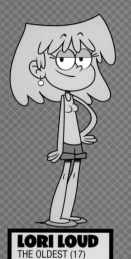

## LORI LOUD
THE OLDEST (17)

As the first-born child of the Loud Clan, Lori sees herself as the boss of all her siblings. She feels she's paved the way for them and deserves extra respect. Her signature traits are rolling her eyes, texting her boyfriend, Bobby, and literally saying "literally" all the time. Because she's the oldest and most experienced sibling, Lori can be a great ally, so it pays to stay on her good side, especially since she can drive.

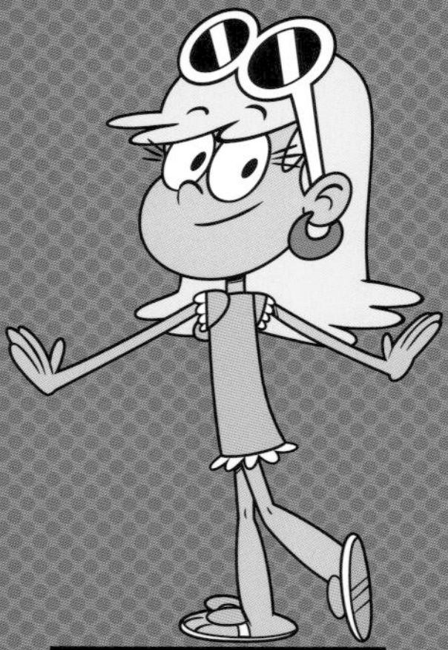

## LENI LOUD
THE FASHIONISTA (16)

Leni spends most of her time designing outfits and accessorizing. She always falls for Luan's pranks, and sometimes walks into walls when she's talking (she's not great at doing two things at once). Leni might be flighty, but she's the sweetest of the Loud siblings and truly has a heart of gold (even though she's pretty sure it's a heart of blood).

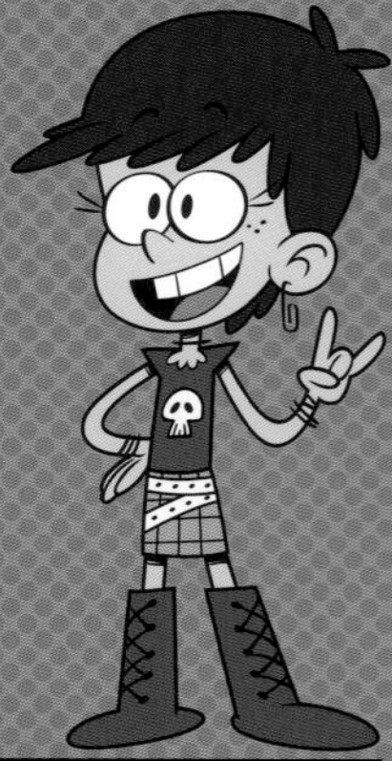

## LUNA LOUD
THE ROCK STAR (15)

Luna is loud, boisterous and freewheeling, and her energy is always cranked to 11. She thinks about music so much that she even talks in song lyrics. On the off-chance she doesn't have her guitar with her, everything can and will be turned into a musical instrument. You can always count on Luna to help out, and she'll do most anything you ask, as long as you're okay with her supplying a rocking guitar accompaniment.

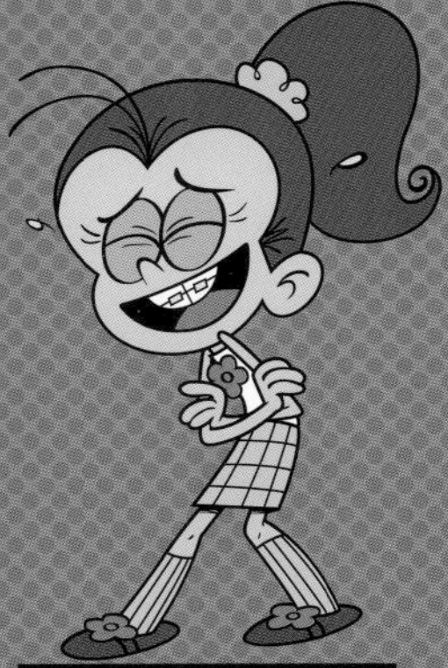

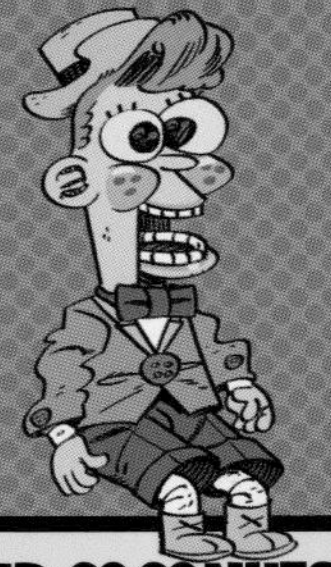

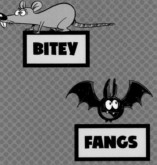

## MR COCONUTS

Luan Loud's wise-cracking dummy.

## LUAN LOUD
THE JOKESTER (14)

Luan's a standup comedienne who provides a nonstop barrage of silly puns. She's big on prop comedy too – squirting flowers and whoopee cushions – so you have to be on your toes whenever she's around. She loves to pull pranks and is a really good ventriloquist – she is often found doing bits with her dummy, Mr. Coconuts. Luan never lets anything get her down; to her, laughter IS the best medicine.

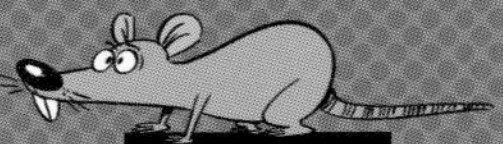

## BITEY

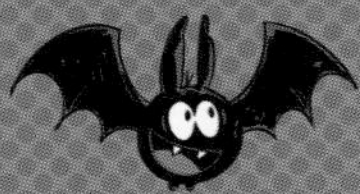

## FANGS

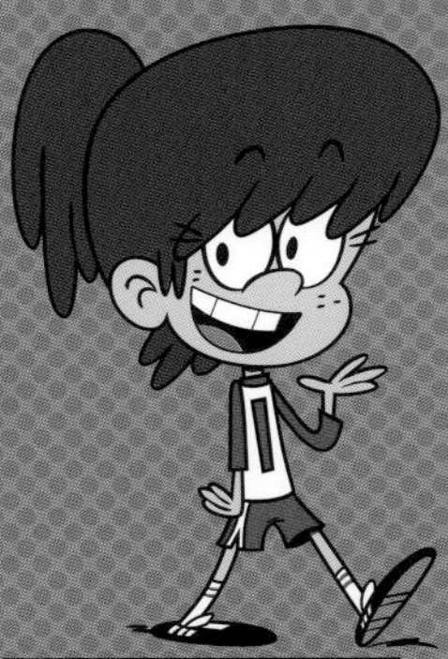

## LYNN LOUD
THE ATHLETE (13)

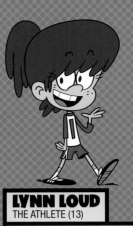

Lynn is athletic and full of energy and is always looking for a teammate. With her, it's all sports all the time. She'll turn anything into a sport. Putting away eggs? Jump shot! Score! Cleaning up the eggs? Slap shot! Score! Lynn is very competitive, but despite her competitive nature, she always tries to just have a good time.

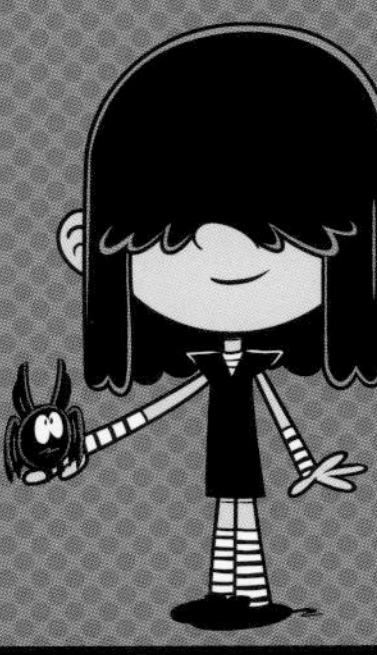

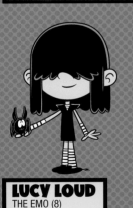

## LUCY LOUD
THE EMO (8)

You can always count on Lucy to give the morbid point of view in any given situation. She is obsessed with all things spooky and dark – funerals, vampires, séances, and the like. She wears mostly black and writes moody poetry. She's usually quiet and keeps to herself. Lucy has a way of mysteriously appearing out of nowhere, and try as they might, her siblings never get used to this.

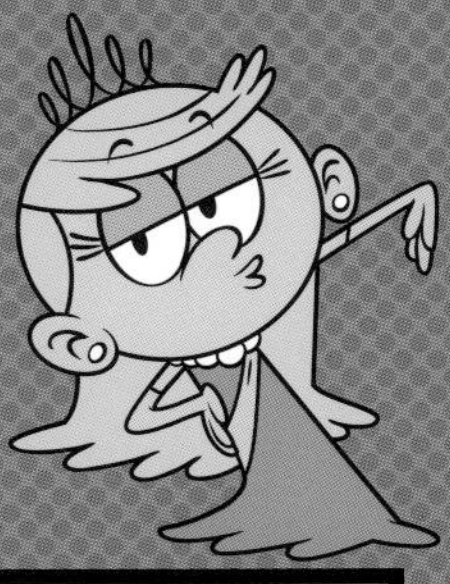

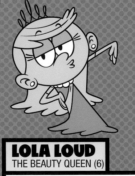

## LOLA LOUD
THE BEAUTY QUEEN (6)

Lola could not be more different from her twin sister, Lana. She's a pageant powerhouse whose interests include glitter, photo shoots, and her own beautiful, beautiful face. But don't let her cute, gap-toothed smile fool you; underneath all the sugar and spice lurks a Machiavellian mastermind. Whatever Lola wants, Lola gets – or else. She's the eyes and ears of the household and never resists an opportunity to tattle on troublemakers. But if you stay on Lola's good side, you've got yourself a fierce ally – and a lifetime supply of free makeovers.

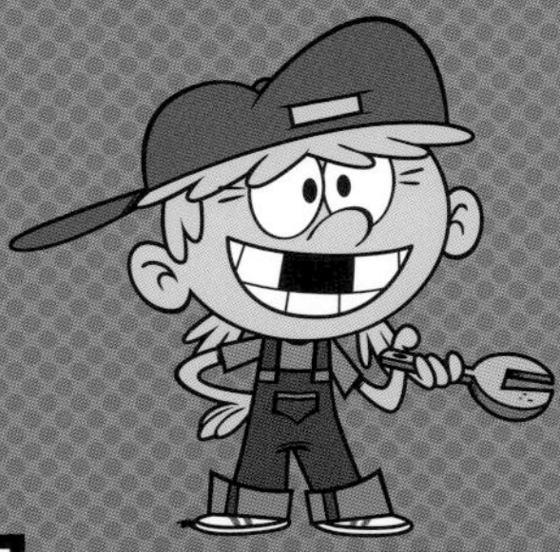

## LANA LOUD
THE TOMBOY (6)

Lana is the rough-and-tumble sparkplug counterpart to her twin sister, Lola. She's all about reptiles, mud pies, and muffler repair. She's the resident Ms. Fix-it and is always ready to lend a hand – the dirtier the job, the better. Need your toilet unclogged? Snake fed? Back-zit popped? Lana's your gal. All she asks in return is a little A-B-C gum, or a handful of kibble (she often sneaks it from the dog bowl).

## LISA LOUD
### THE GENIUS (4)

Lisa is smarter than the rest of her siblings combined. She'll most likely be a rocket scientist, or a brain surgeon, or an evil genius who takes over the world. Lisa spends most of her time working in her lab (the family has gotten used to the explosions), and says her research leaves little time for frivolous human pursuits like "playing" or "getting haircuts." That said, she's always there to help with a homework question, or to explain why the sky is blue, or to point out the structural flaws in someone's pillow fort. Lisa says it's the least she can do for her favorite test subjects, er, siblings.

## LILY LOUD
### THE BABY (15 MONTHS)

Lily is a giggly, drooly, diaper-ditching free spirit, affectionately known as "the poop machine." You can't keep a nappy on this kid – she's like a teething Houdini. But even when Lily's running wild, dropping rancid diaper bombs, or drooling all over the remote, she always brings a smile to everyone's face (and a clothespin to their nose). Lily is everyone's favorite little buddy, and the whole family loves her unconditionally.

## CHARLES

## WALT

## CLIFF

## GEO

## RITA LOUD

Mother to the eleven Loud kids, Mom (Rita Loud) wears many different hats. She's a chauffeur, homework-checker and barf-cleaner-upper all rolled into one. She's always there for her kids and ready to jump into action during a crisis, whether it's a fight between the twins or Leni's missing shoe. When she's not chasing the kids around or at her day job as a dental hygienist for Dr. Feinstein, Mom pursues her passion: writing. She also loves taking on house projects and is very handy with tools (guess that's where Lana gets it from). Between writing, working and being a mom, her days are always hectic but she wouldn't have it any other way.

## LYNN LOUD SR.

Dad (Lynn Loud Sr.) is a fun-loving, upbeat aspiring chef. A kid-at-heart, he's not above taking part in the kids' zany schemes. In addition to cooking, Dad loves his van, playing the cowbell and making puns. Before meeting Mom, Dad spent a semester in England and has been obsessed with British culture ever since – and sometimes "accidentally" slips into a British accent. When Dad's not wrangling the kids, he's pursuing his dream of opening his own restaurant where he hopes to make his "Lynn-sagnas" world-famous.

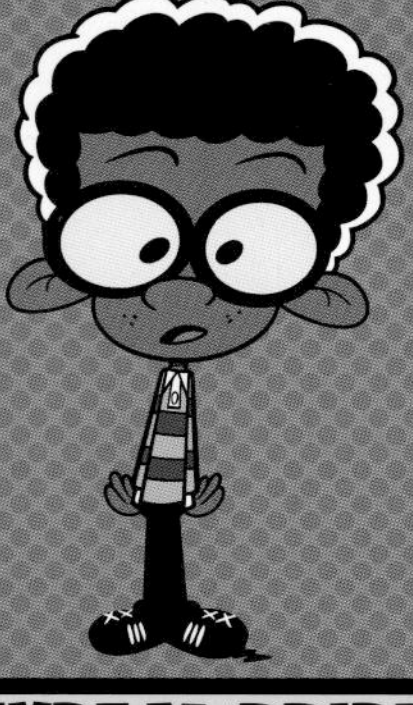

## CLYDE McBRIDE
THE BEST FRIEND (11)

Clyde is Lincoln's partner in crime. He's always willing to go along with Lincoln's crazy schemes (even if he sees the flaws in them up-front). Lincoln and Clyde are two peas in a pod and share pretty much all of the same tastes in movies, comics, TV shows, toys—you name it. As an only child, Clyde envies Lincoln—how cool would it be to always have siblings around to talk to? But since Clyde spends so much time at the Loud household, he's almost an honorary sibling anyway.

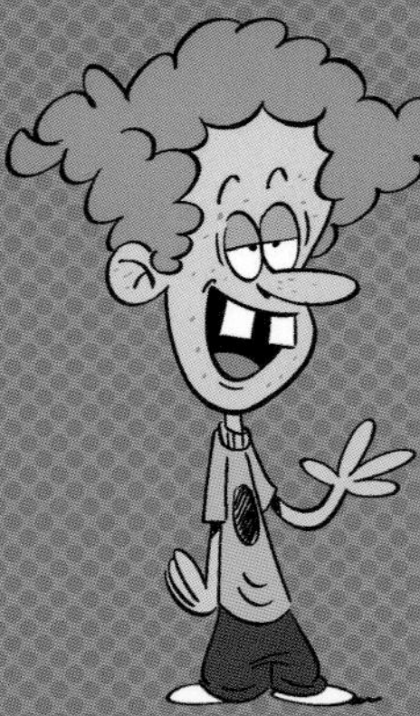

## RUSTY SPOKES

Rusty is a self-proclaimed ladies' man who's always the first to dish out girl advice—even though he's never been on an actual date. His dad owns a suit rental service, so occasionally Rusty can hook the gang up with some dapper duds—just as long as no one gets anything dirty.

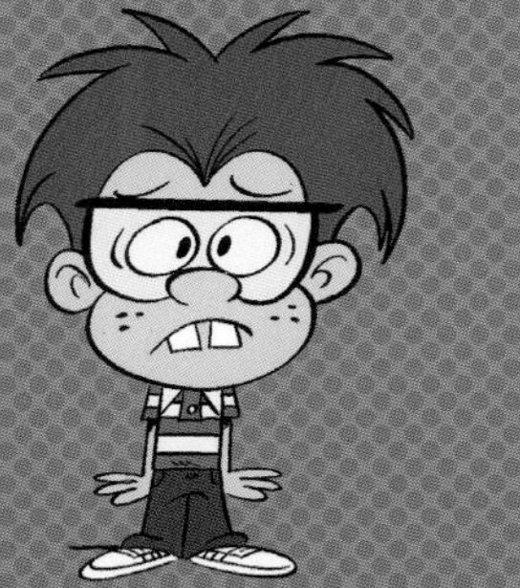

## ZACH GURDLE

Zach is a self-admitted nerd who's obsessed with aliens and conspiracy theories. He lives between a freeway and a circus, so the chaos of the Loud House doesn't faze him. He and Rusty occasionally butt heads, but deep down, it's all love.

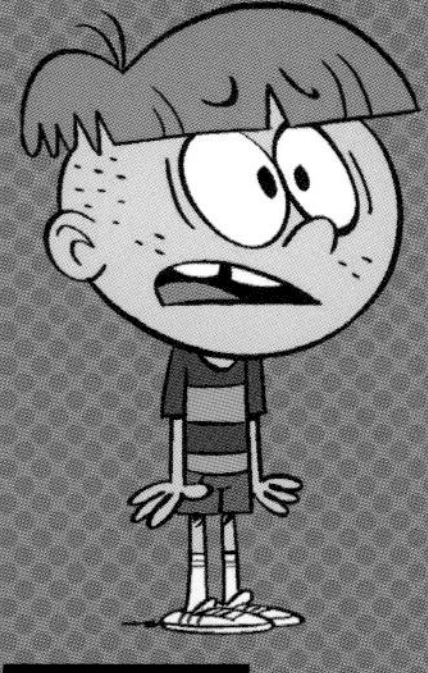

## LIAM

Liam is an enthusiastic, sweet-natured farm boy full of down-home wisdom. He loves hanging out with his Mee Maw, wrestling his prize pig Virginia, and sharing his farm-to-table produce with the rest of the gang.

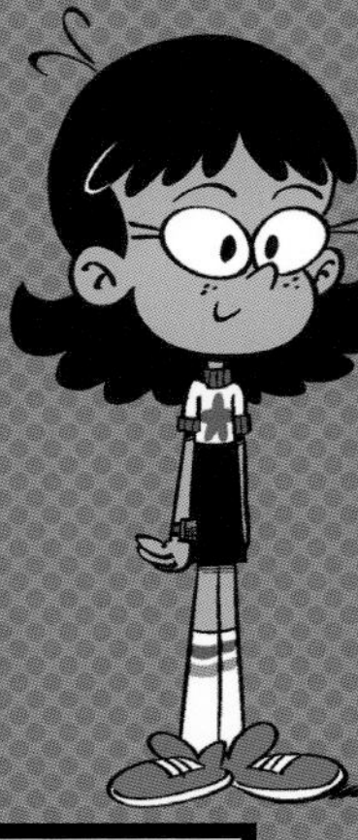

## STELLA

Stella, 11, is a quirky, carefree girl who's new to Royal Woods. She has tons of interests, like trying on wigs, playing laser tag, eating curly fries, and hanging with her friends. But what she loves the most is tech — she always wants to dismantle electronics and put them back together again.

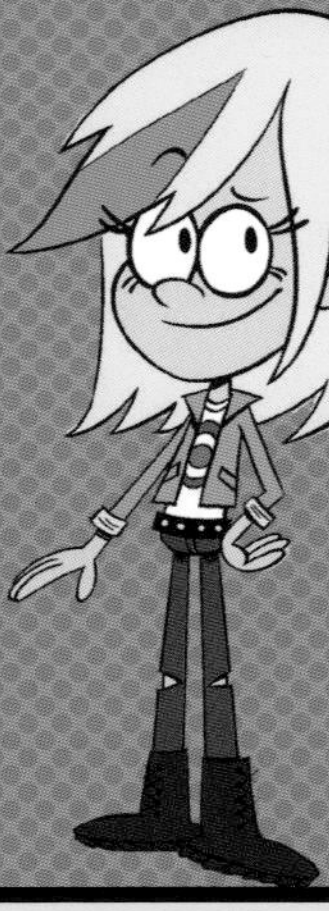

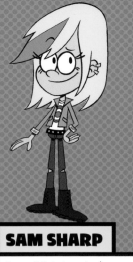

## SAM SHARP

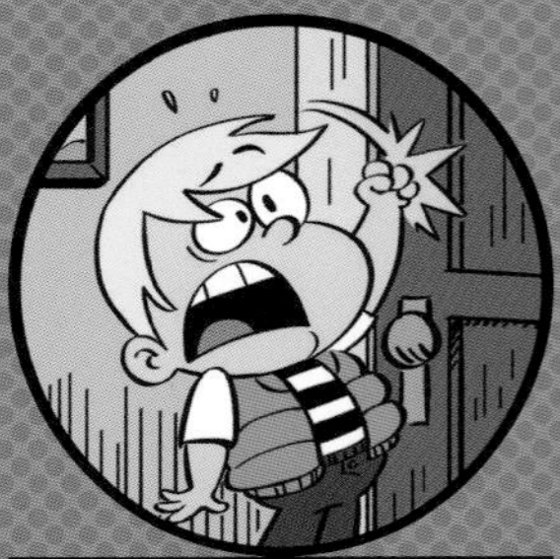

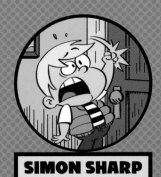

## SIMON SHARP

Sam, 15, is Luna's classmate and good friend, who Luna has a crush on. Sam is all about the music – she loves to play guitar and write and compose music. Her favorite genre is rock and roll but she appreciates all good tunes. Unlike Luna, Sam only has one brother, Simon, but she thinks even one sibling provides enough chaos for her.

## LENI'S COWORKER FRIENDS

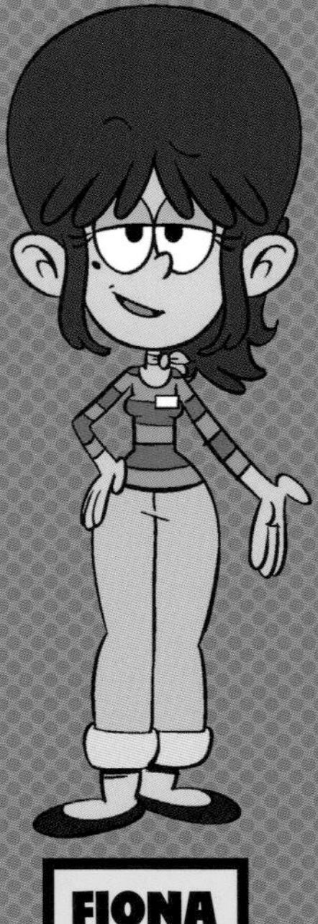

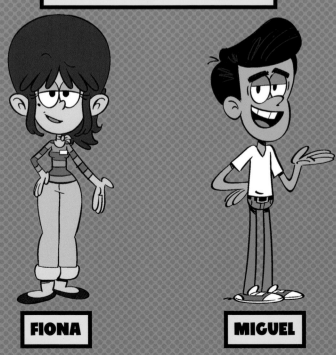

### FIONA

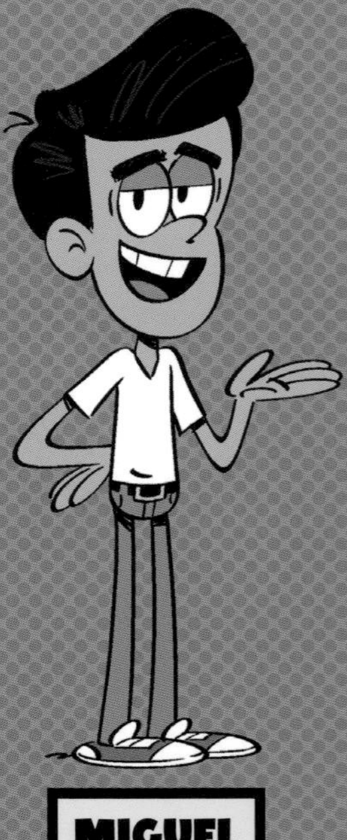

### MIGUEL

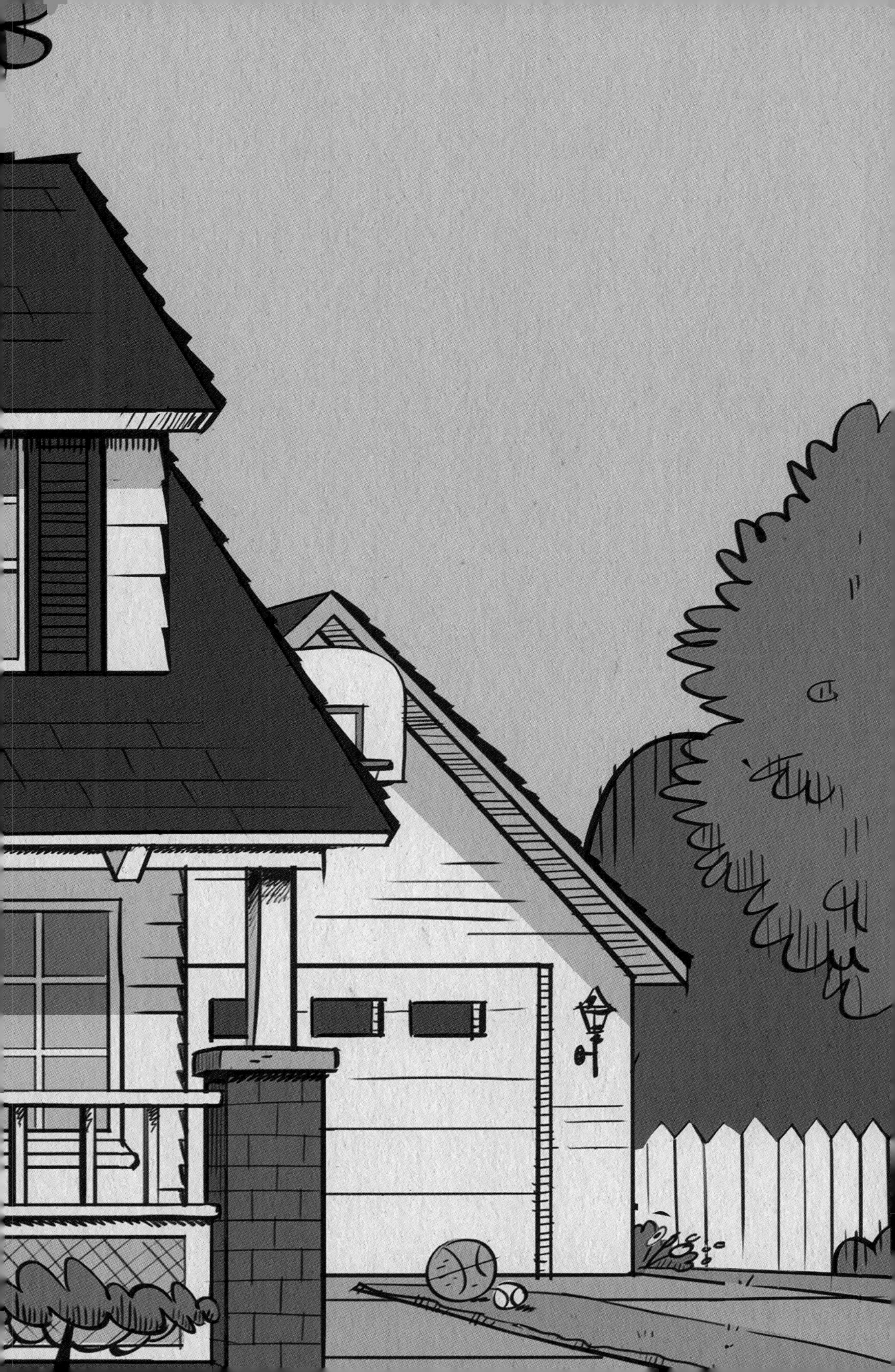

# "THE HAUNTED HOUSE"

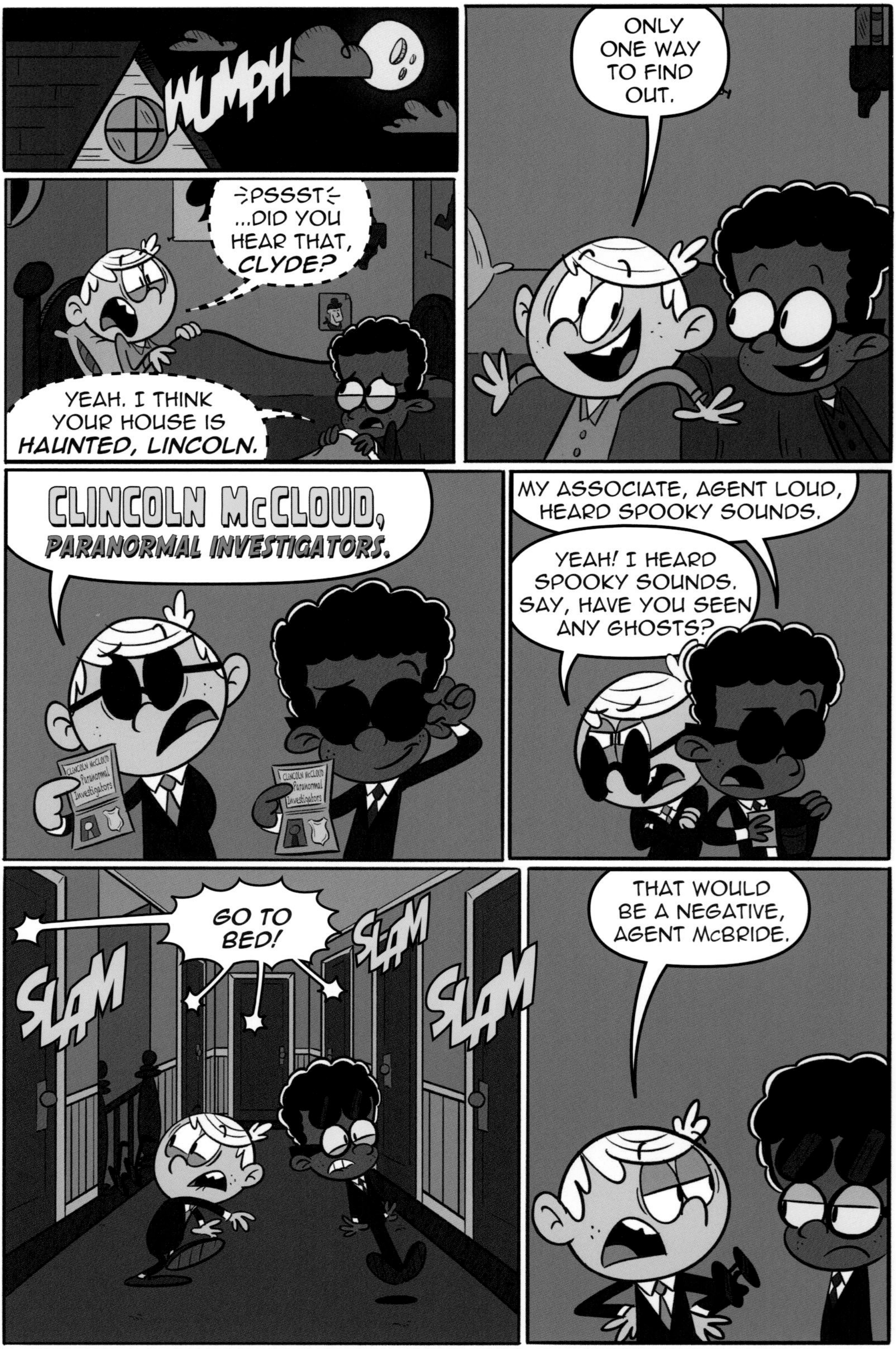
WUMPH
PSSST ...DID YOU HEAR THAT, CLYDE?
YEAH. I THINK YOUR HOUSE IS HAUNTED, LINCOLN.
ONLY ONE WAY TO FIND OUT.
CLINCOLN McCLOUD, PARANORMAL INVESTIGATORS.
MY ASSOCIATE, AGENT LOUD, HEARD SPOOKY SOUNDS.
YEAH! I HEARD SPOOKY SOUNDS. SAY, HAVE YOU SEEN ANY GHOSTS?
GO TO BED!
SLAM
SLAM
SLAM
THAT WOULD BE A NEGATIVE, AGENT McBRIDE.

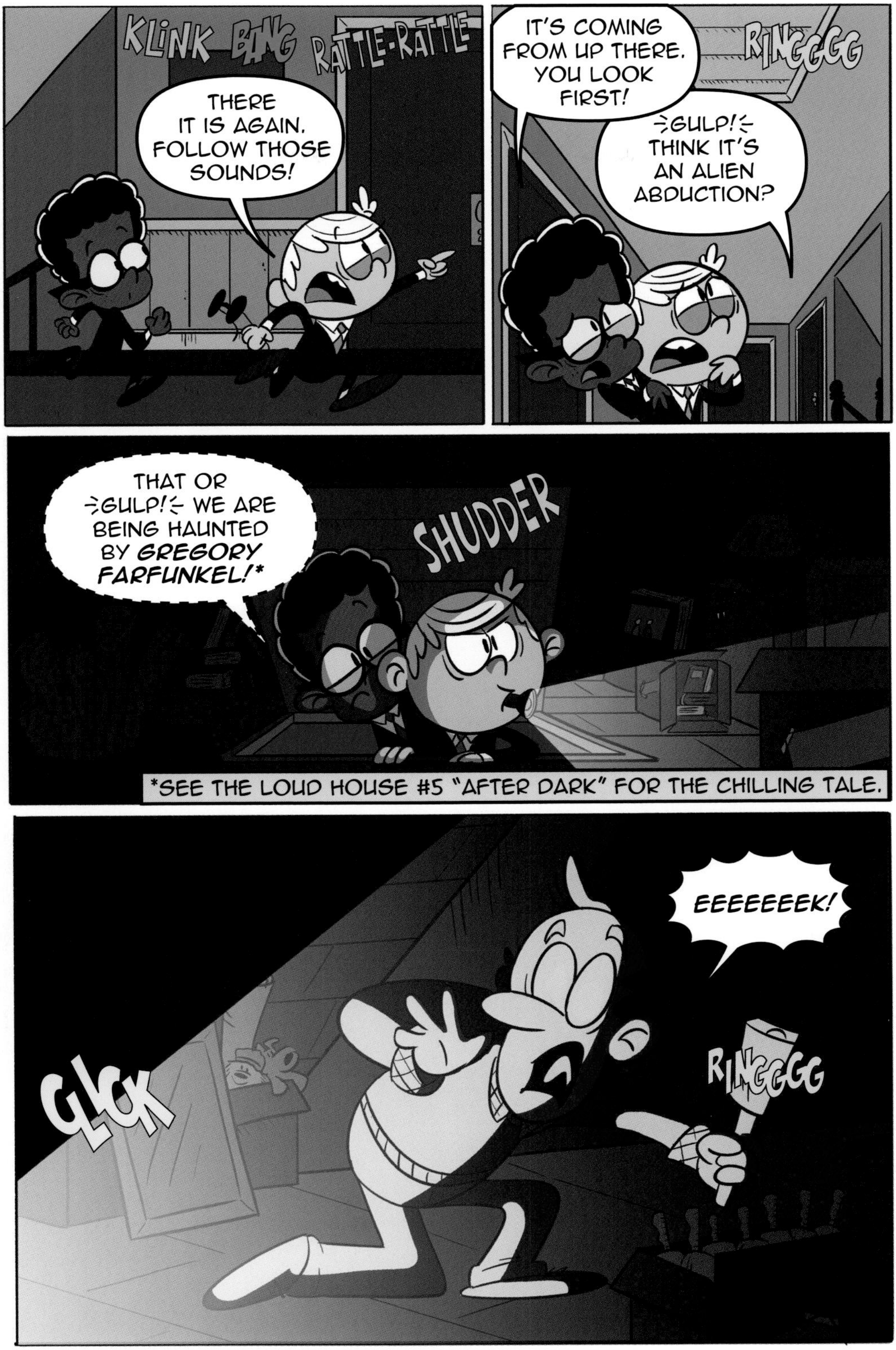
KLINK BANG RATTLE-RATTLE
THERE IT IS AGAIN. FOLLOW THOSE SOUNDS!
IT'S COMING FROM UP THERE. YOU LOOK FIRST!
RINGGGG
GULP! THINK IT'S AN ALIEN ABDUCTION?
THAT OR GULP! WE ARE BEING HAUNTED BY GREGORY FARFUNKEL!*
SHUDDER
*SEE THE LOUD HOUSE #5 "AFTER DARK" FOR THE CHILLING TALE.
CLICK
EEEEEEEK!
RINGGGG

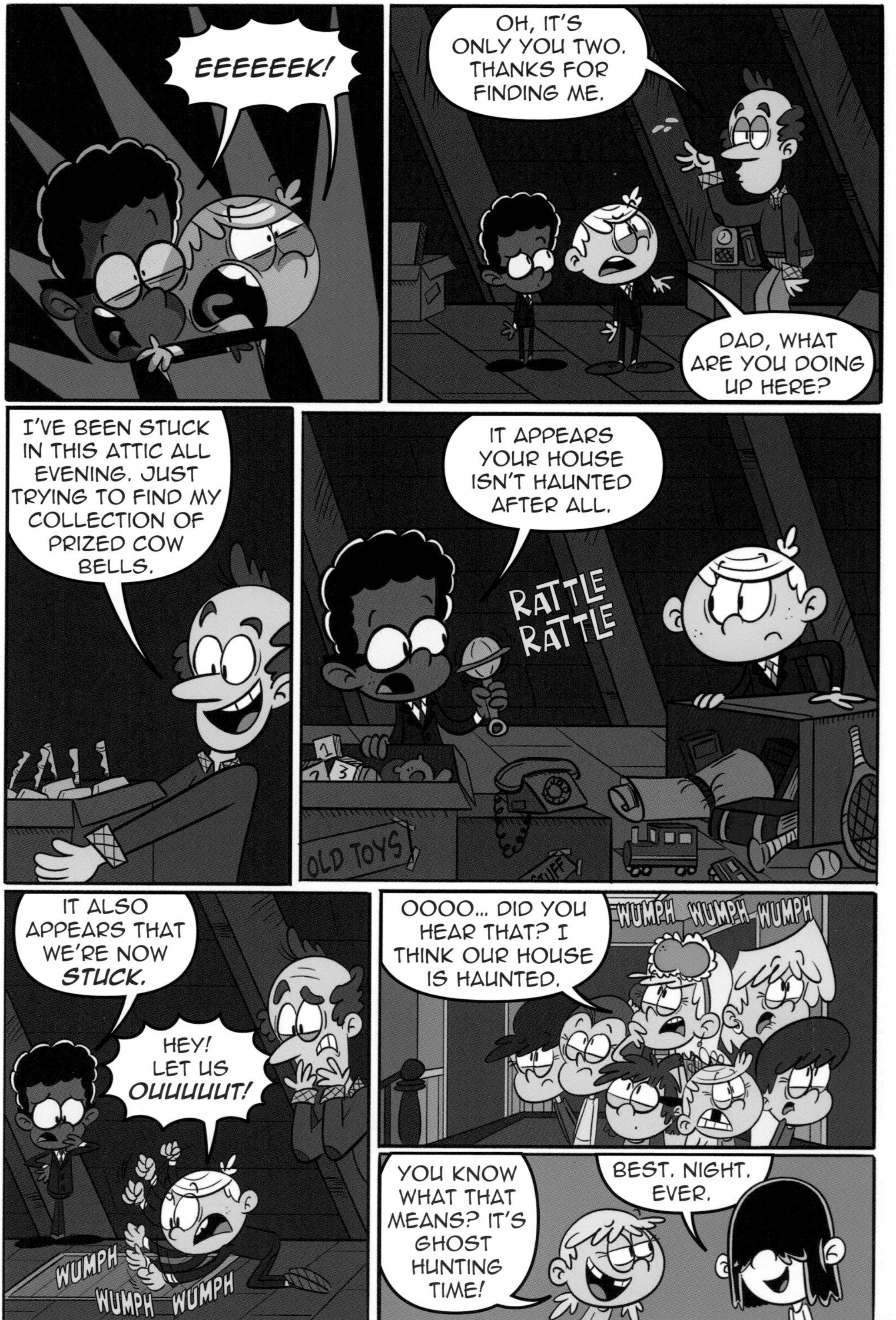
EEEEEEK!
OH, IT'S ONLY YOU TWO. THANKS FOR FINDING ME.
DAD, WHAT ARE YOU DOING UP HERE?
I'VE BEEN STUCK IN THIS ATTIC ALL EVENING. JUST TRYING TO FIND MY COLLECTION OF PRIZED COW BELLS.
IT APPEARS YOUR HOUSE ISN'T HAUNTED AFTER ALL.
RATTLE RATTLE
OLD TOYS
IT ALSO APPEARS THAT WE'RE NOW STUCK.
HEY! LET US OUUUUUT!
WUMPH WUMPH WUMPH
OOOO... DID YOU HEAR THAT? I THINK OUR HOUSE IS HAUNTED.
WUMPH WUMPH WUMPH
YOU KNOW WHAT THAT MEANS? IT'S GHOST HUNTING TIME!
BEST. NIGHT. EVER.
END?

# "LUCY OF MELANCHOLIA"

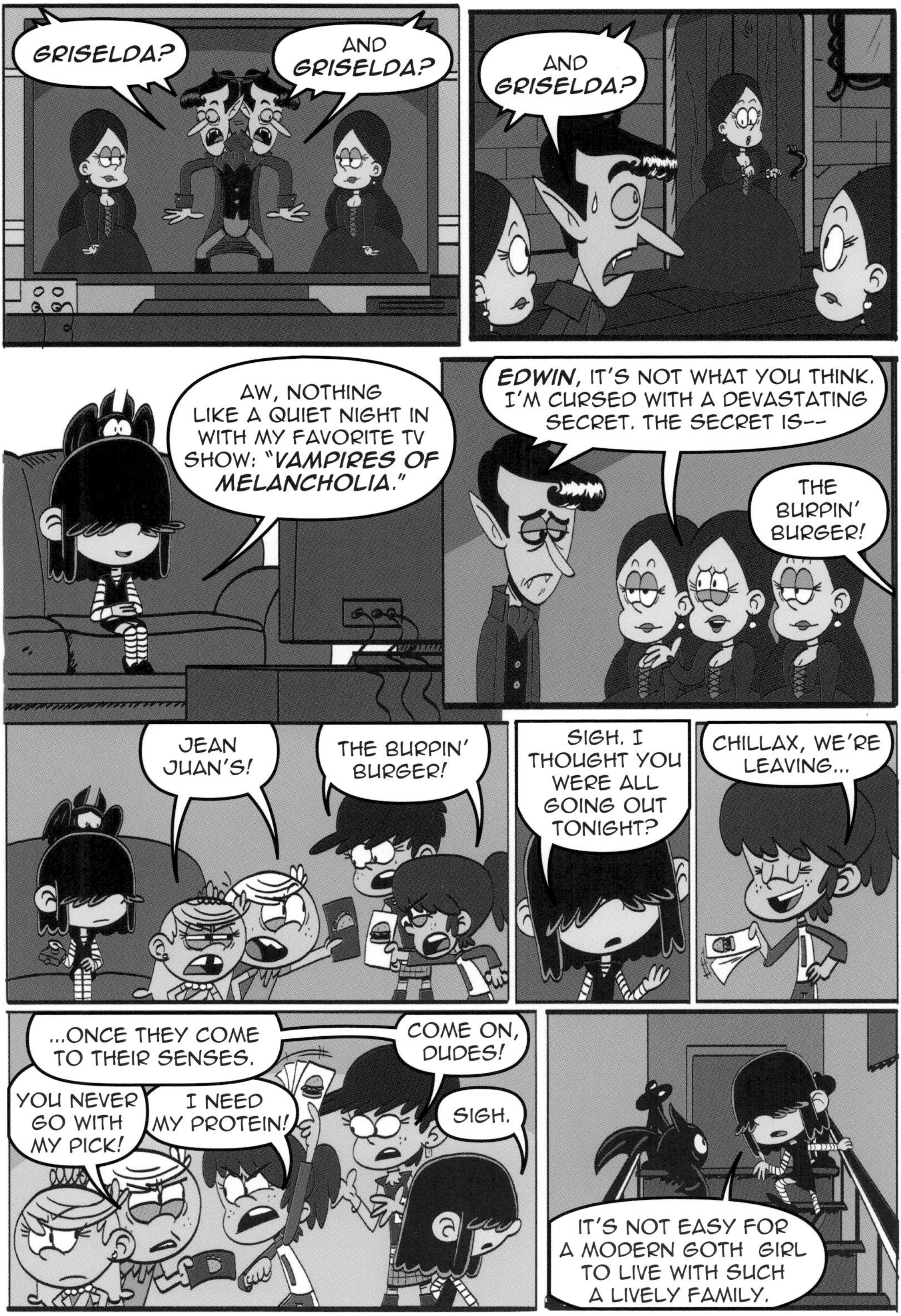
GRISELDA?
AND GRISELDA?
AND GRISELDA?
AW, NOTHING LIKE A QUIET NIGHT IN WITH MY FAVORITE TV SHOW: "VAMPIRES OF MELANCHOLIA."
EDWIN, IT'S NOT WHAT YOU THINK. I'M CURSED WITH A DEVASTATING SECRET. THE SECRET IS--
THE BURPIN' BURGER!
JEAN JUAN'S!
THE BURPIN' BURGER!
SIGH. I THOUGHT YOU WERE ALL GOING OUT TONIGHT?
CHILLAX, WE'RE LEAVING...
...ONCE THEY COME TO THEIR SENSES.
COME ON, DUDES!
YOU NEVER GO WITH MY PICK!
I NEED MY PROTEIN!
SIGH.
IT'S NOT EASY FOR A MODERN GOTH GIRL TO LIVE WITH SUCH A LIVELY FAMILY.

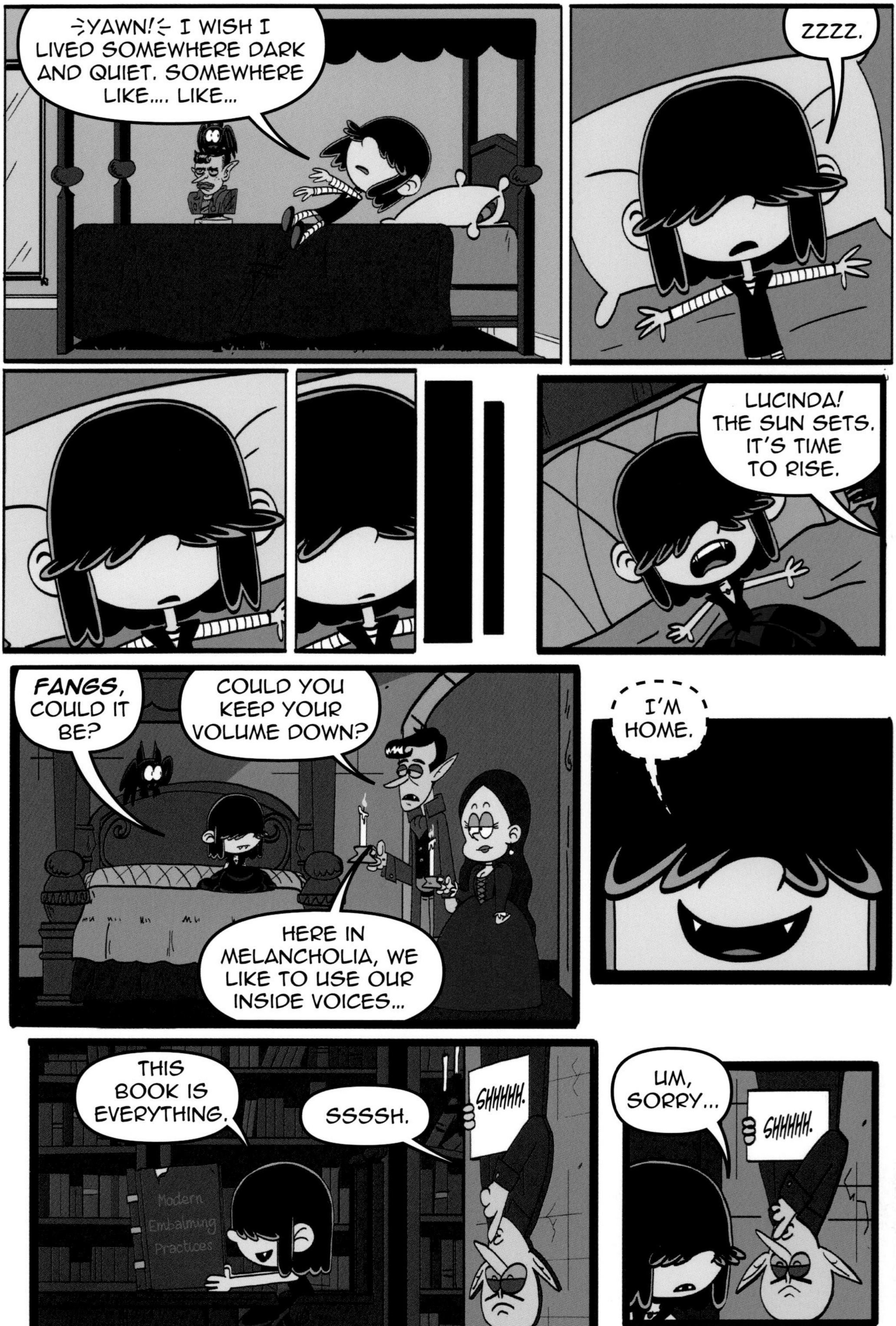
⁼YAWN!⁼ I WISH I LIVED SOMEWHERE DARK AND QUIET. SOMEWHERE LIKE.... LIKE...
ZZZZ.
LUCINDA! THE SUN SETS. IT'S TIME TO RISE.
FANGS, COULD IT BE?
COULD YOU KEEP YOUR VOLUME DOWN?
HERE IN MELANCHOLIA, WE LIKE TO USE OUR INSIDE VOICES...
I'M HOME.
THIS BOOK IS EVERYTHING.
Modern Embalming Practices
SSSSH.
SHHHHH.
UM, SORRY...
SHHHHH.

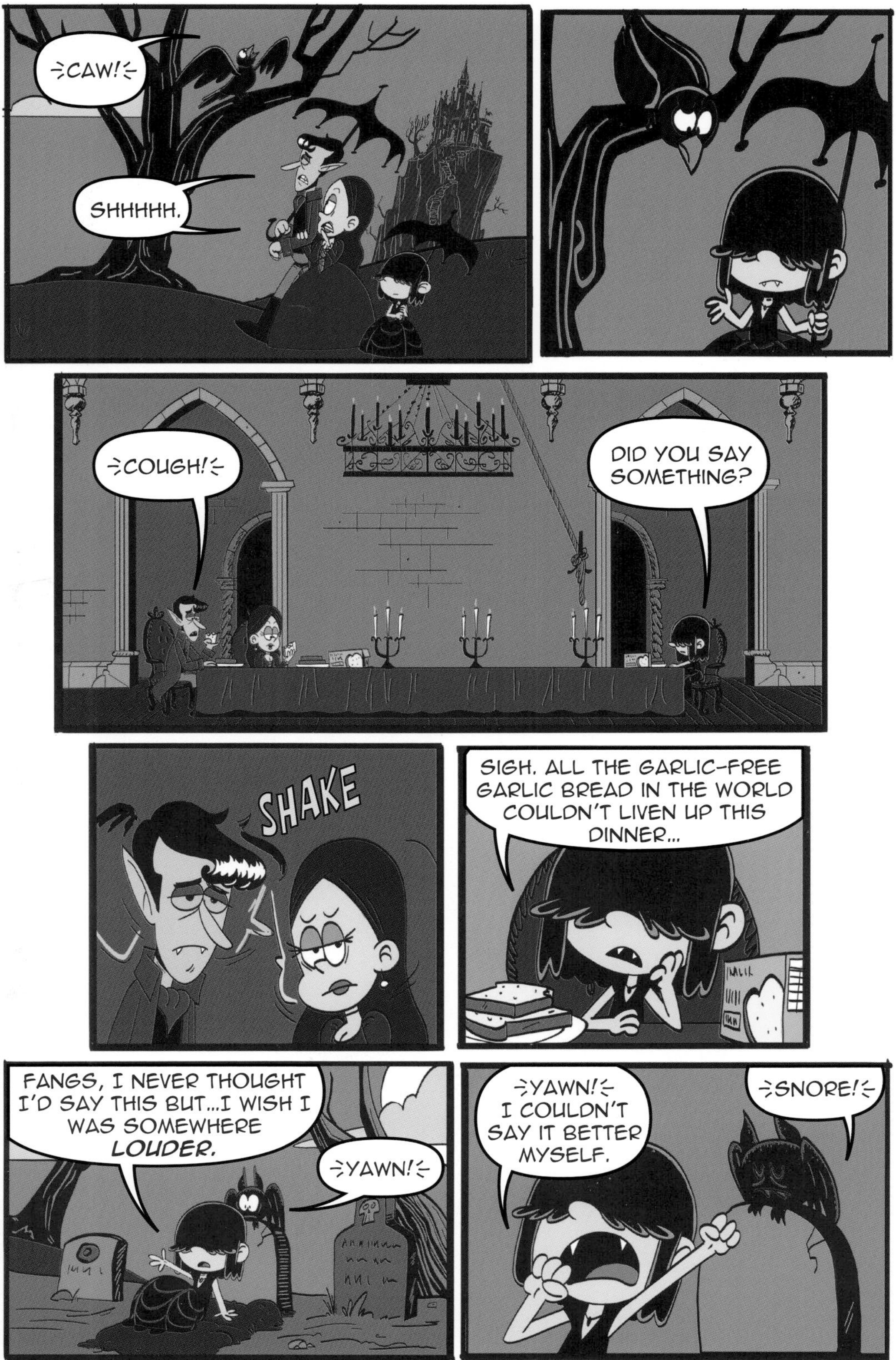

CAW!
SHHHHH.
COUGH!
DID YOU SAY SOMETHING?
SHAKE
SIGH. ALL THE GARLIC-FREE GARLIC BREAD IN THE WORLD COULDN'T LIVEN UP THIS DINNER...
FANGS, I NEVER THOUGHT I'D SAY THIS BUT...I WISH I WAS SOMEWHERE *LOUDER.*
YAWN!
YAWN! I COULDN'T SAY IT BETTER MYSELF.
SNORE!

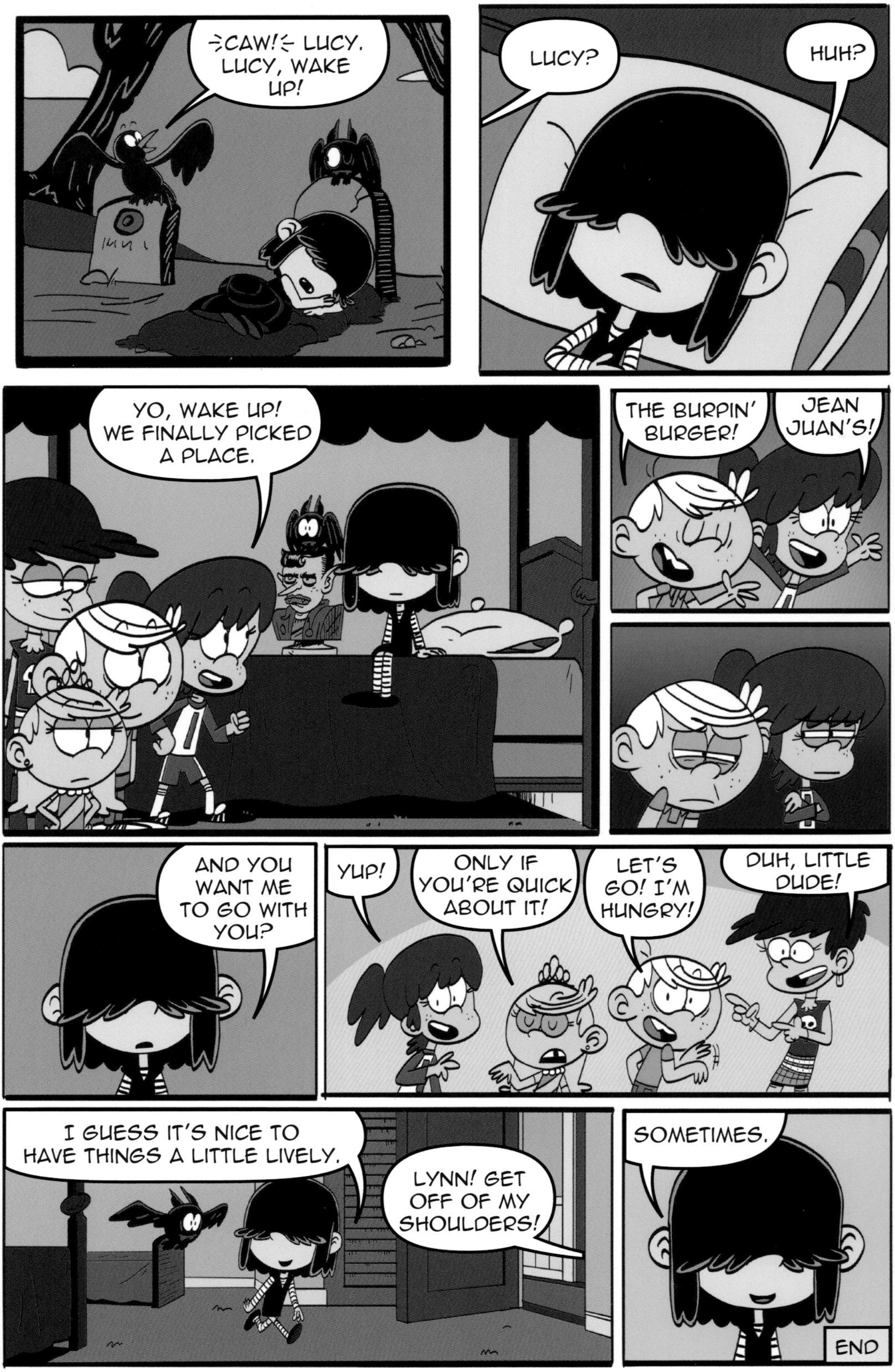

CAW! LUCY. LUCY, WAKE UP!
LUCY?
HUH?
YO, WAKE UP! WE FINALLY PICKED A PLACE.
THE BURPIN' BURGER!
JEAN JUAN'S!
AND YOU WANT ME TO GO WITH YOU?
YUP!
ONLY IF YOU'RE QUICK ABOUT IT!
LET'S GO! I'M HUNGRY!
DUH, LITTLE DUDE!
I GUESS IT'S NICE TO HAVE THINGS A LITTLE LIVELY.
LYNN! GET OFF OF MY SHOULDERS!
SOMETIMES.
END

# "ROCKIN' ROUTINE"

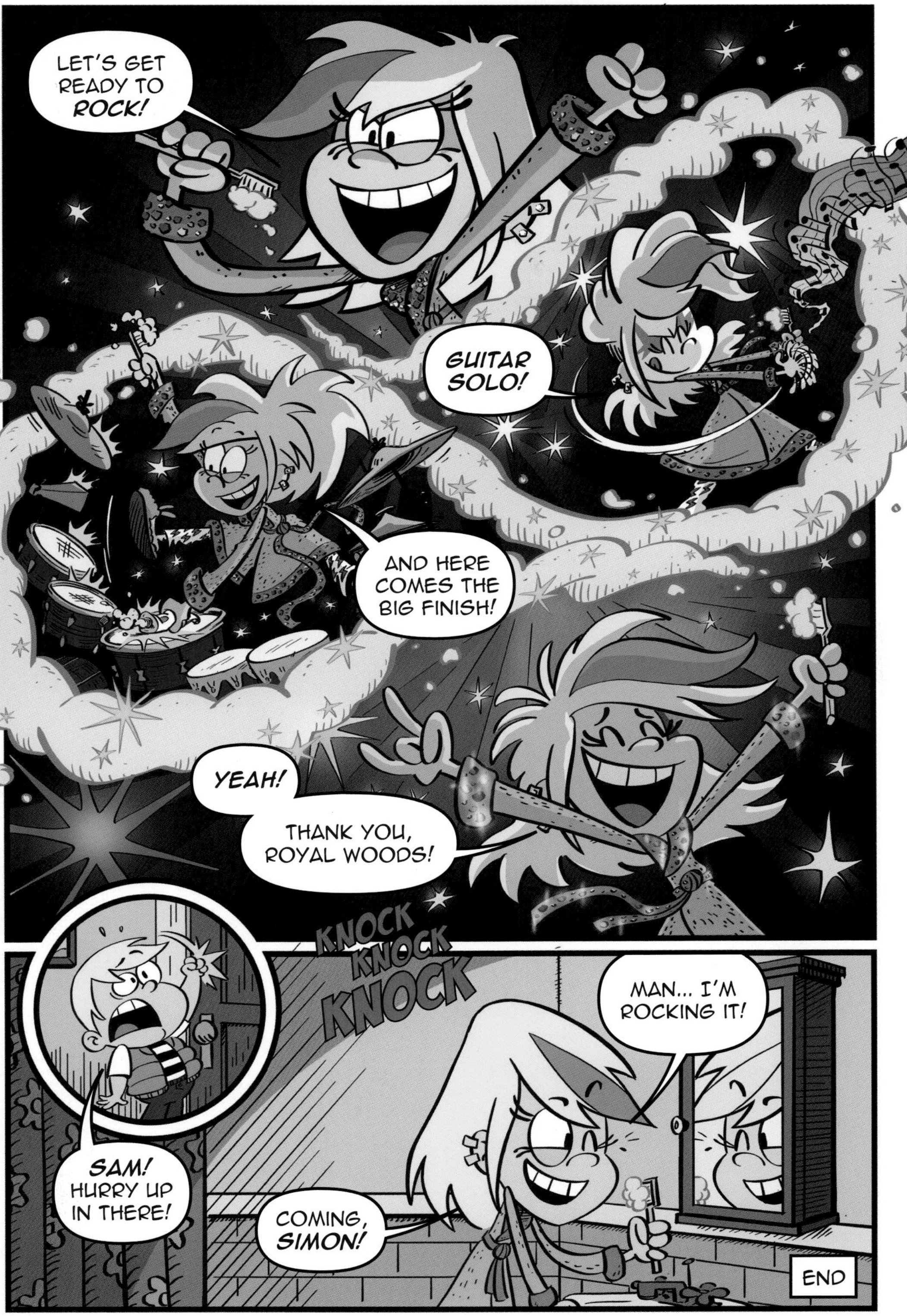
LET'S GET READY TO ROCK!
GUITAR SOLO!
AND HERE COMES THE BIG FINISH!
YEAH!
THANK YOU, ROYAL WOODS!
KNOCK KNOCK KNOCK
SAM! HURRY UP IN THERE!
COMING, SIMON!
MAN... I'M ROCKING IT!
END

# "NONE CHUCKED"

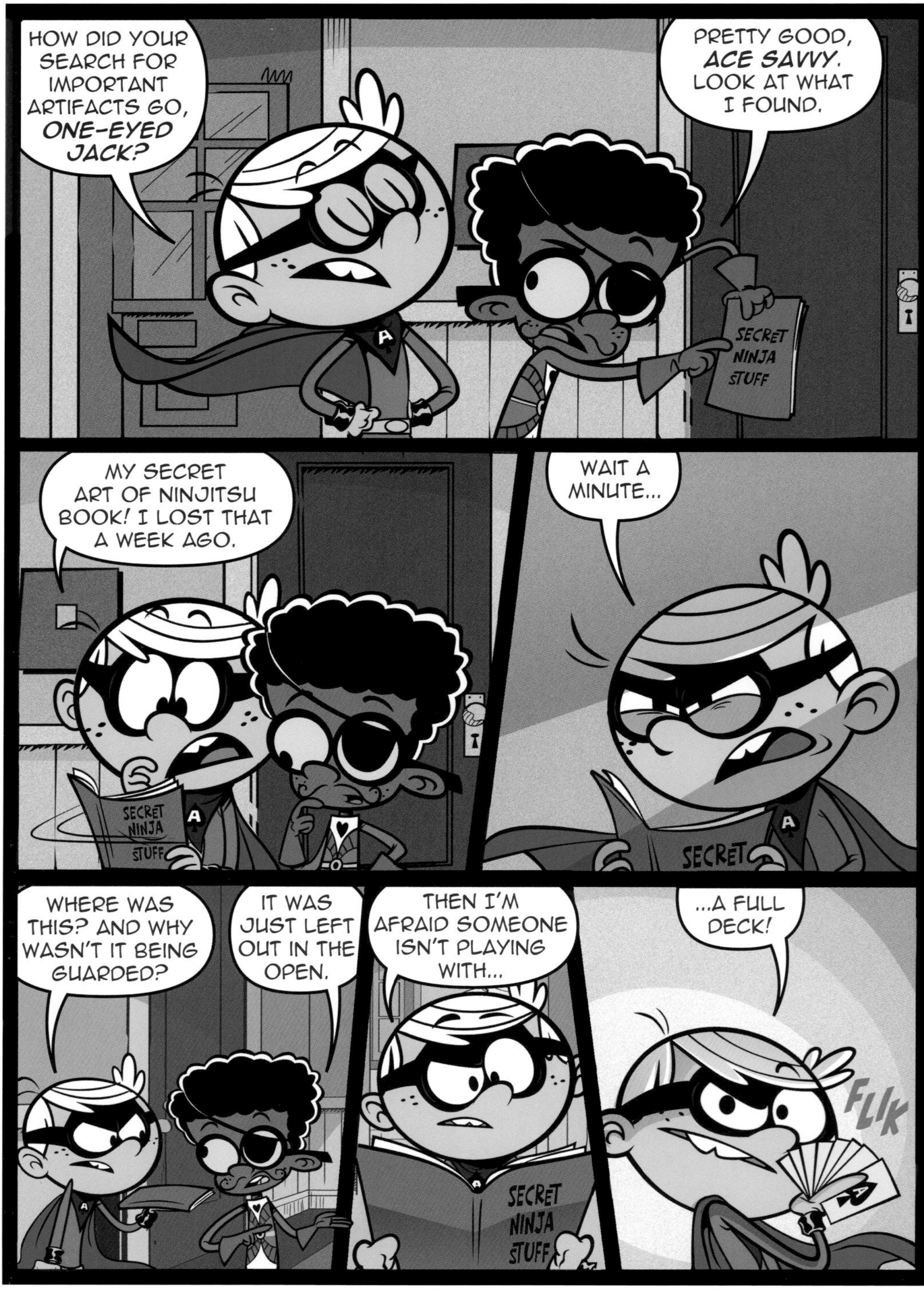
HOW DID YOUR SEARCH FOR IMPORTANT ARTIFACTS GO, *ONE-EYED JACK?*
PRETTY GOOD, *ACE SAVVY*. LOOK AT WHAT I FOUND.
SECRET NINJA STUFF
MY SECRET ART OF NINJITSU BOOK! I LOST THAT A WEEK AGO.
SECRET NINJA STUFF
WAIT A MINUTE...
SECRET
WHERE WAS THIS? AND WHY WASN'T IT BEING GUARDED?
IT WAS JUST LEFT OUT IN THE OPEN.
THEN I'M AFRAID SOMEONE ISN'T PLAYING WITH...
SECRET NINJA STUFF
...A FULL DECK!
FLIK

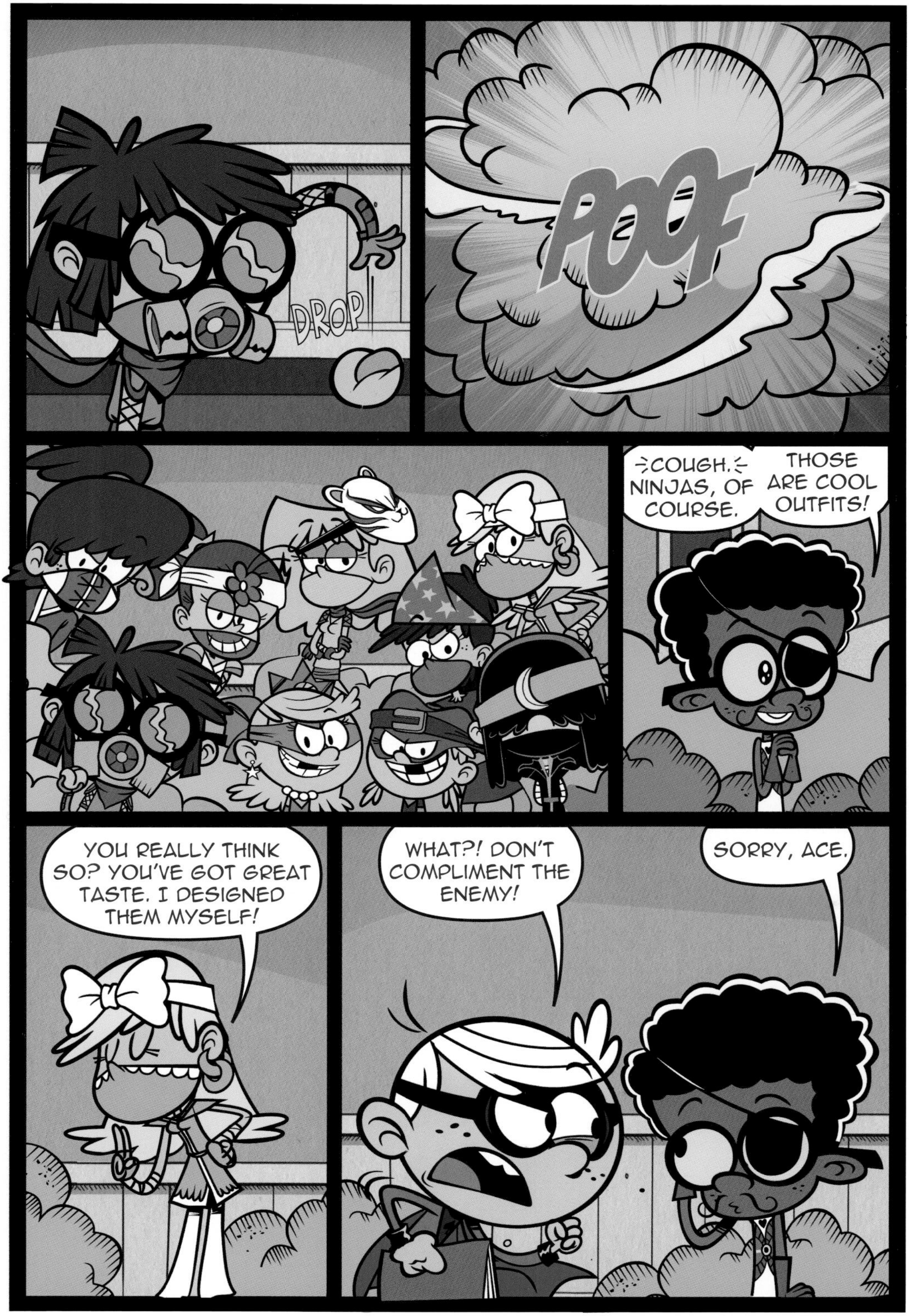
DROP
POOF
*COUGH.* NINJAS, OF COURSE.
THOSE ARE COOL OUTFITS!
YOU REALLY THINK SO? YOU'VE GOT GREAT TASTE. I DESIGNED THEM MYSELF!
WHAT?! DON'T COMPLIMENT THE ENEMY!
SORRY, ACE.

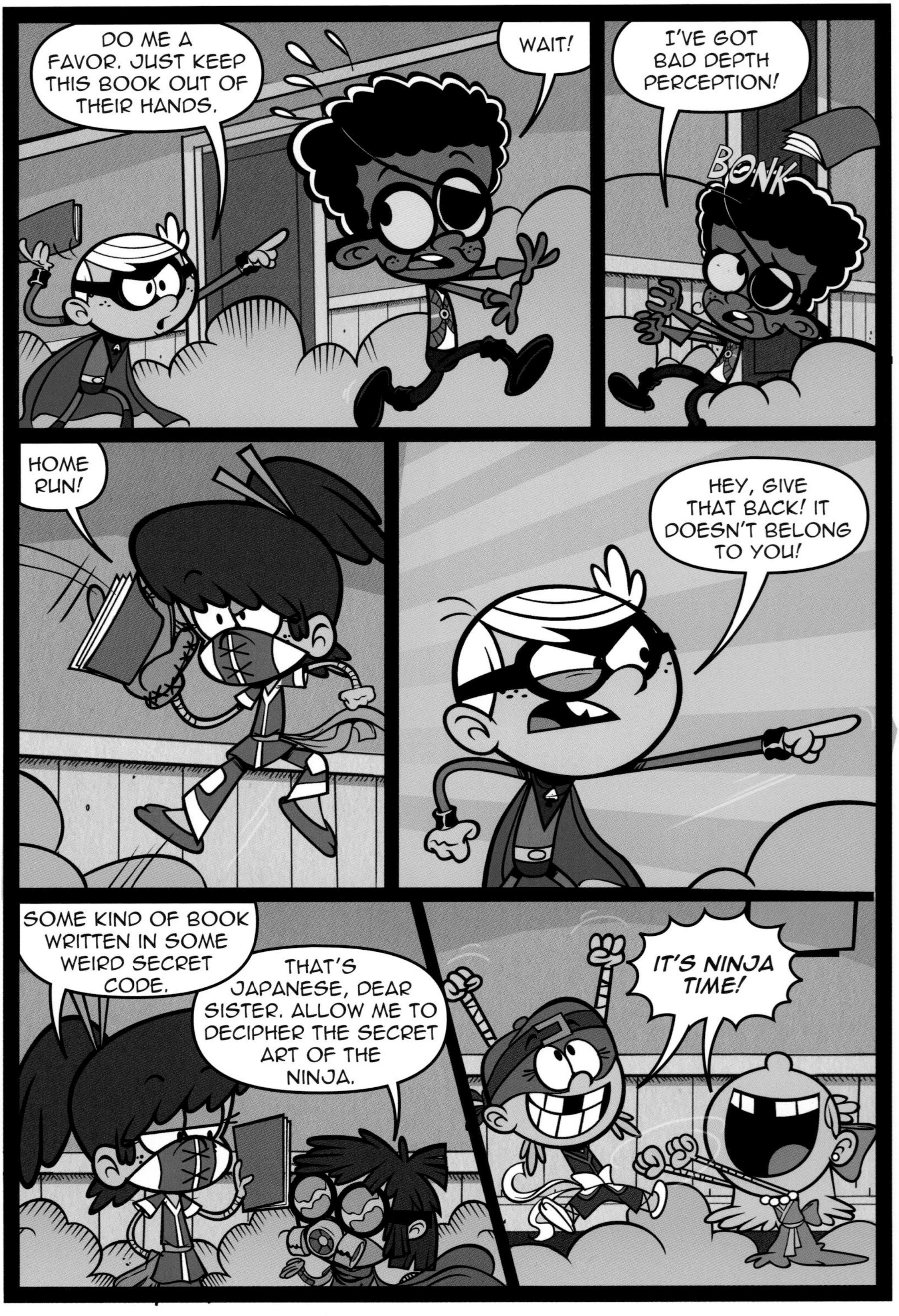
DO ME A FAVOR. JUST KEEP THIS BOOK OUT OF THEIR HANDS.
WAIT!
I'VE GOT BAD DEPTH PERCEPTION!
BONK
HOME RUN!
HEY, GIVE THAT BACK! IT DOESN'T BELONG TO YOU!
SOME KIND OF BOOK WRITTEN IN SOME WEIRD SECRET CODE.
THAT'S JAPANESE, DEAR SISTER. ALLOW ME TO DECIPHER THE SECRET ART OF THE NINJA.
IT'S NINJA TIME!

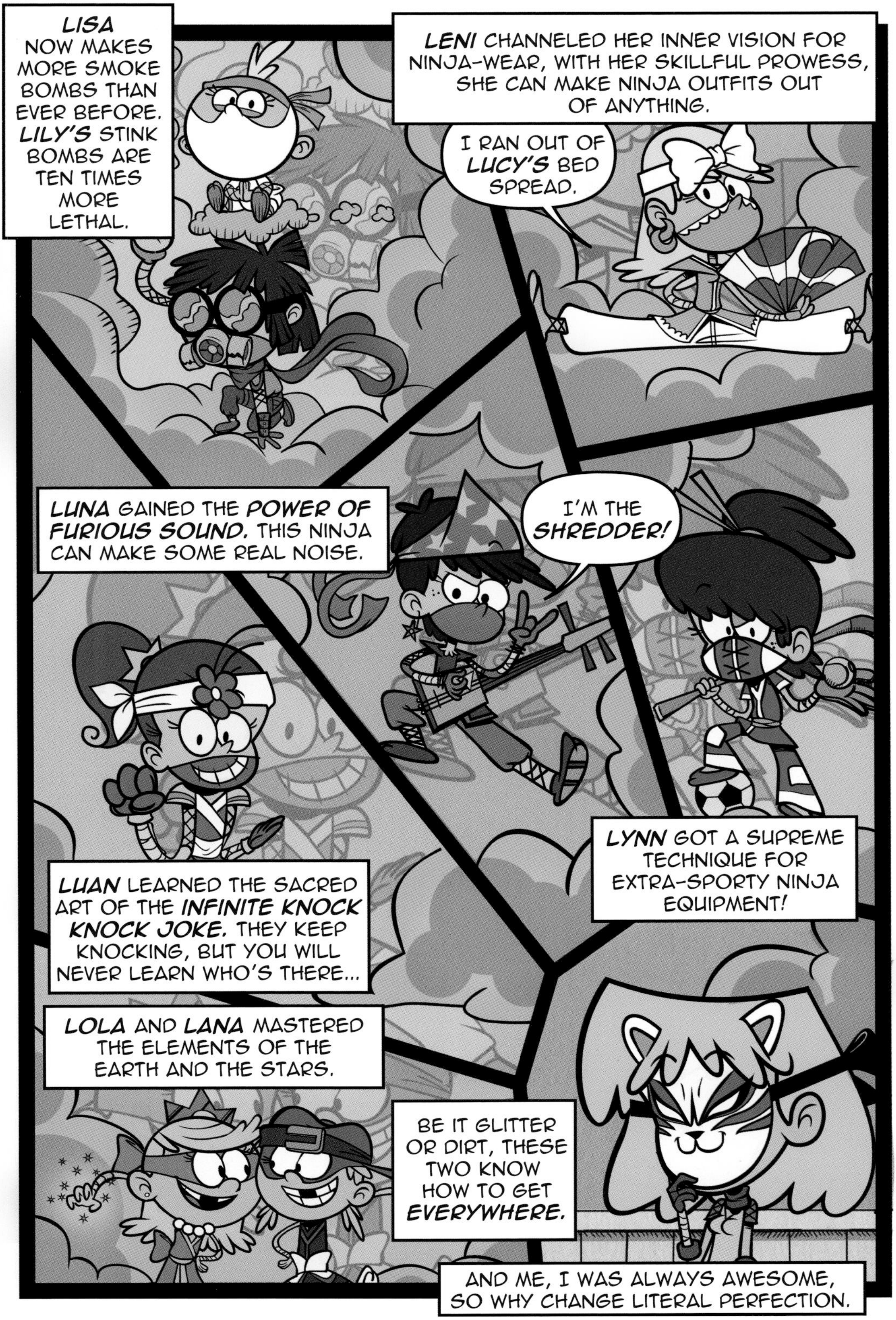
LISA NOW MAKES MORE SMOKE BOMBS THAN EVER BEFORE. LILY'S STINK BOMBS ARE TEN TIMES MORE LETHAL.
LENI CHANNELED HER INNER VISION FOR NINJA-WEAR, WITH HER SKILLFUL PROWESS, SHE CAN MAKE NINJA OUTFITS OUT OF ANYTHING.
I RAN OUT OF LUCY'S BED SPREAD.
LUNA GAINED THE POWER OF FURIOUS SOUND. THIS NINJA CAN MAKE SOME REAL NOISE.
I'M THE SHREDDER!
LYNN GOT A SUPREME TECHNIQUE FOR EXTRA-SPORTY NINJA EQUIPMENT!
LUAN LEARNED THE SACRED ART OF THE INFINITE KNOCK KNOCK JOKE. THEY KEEP KNOCKING, BUT YOU WILL NEVER LEARN WHO'S THERE...
LOLA AND LANA MASTERED THE ELEMENTS OF THE EARTH AND THE STARS.
BE IT GLITTER OR DIRT, THESE TWO KNOW HOW TO GET EVERYWHERE.
AND ME, I WAS ALWAYS AWESOME, SO WHY CHANGE LITERAL PERFECTION.

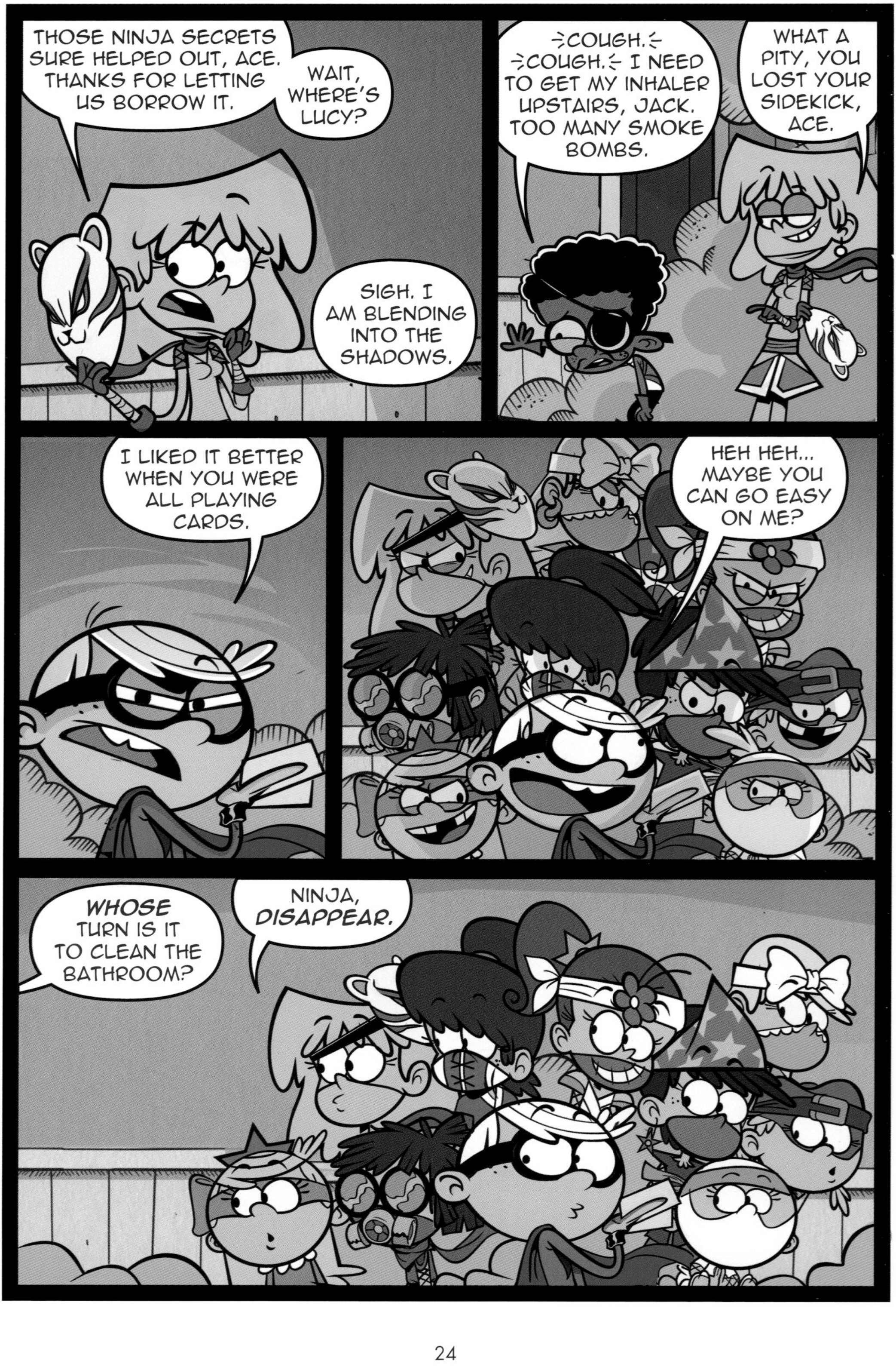
THOSE NINJA SECRETS SURE HELPED OUT, ACE. THANKS FOR LETTING US BORROW IT.
WAIT, WHERE'S LUCY?
SIGH. I AM BLENDING INTO THE SHADOWS.
*COUGH.* *COUGH.* I NEED TO GET MY INHALER UPSTAIRS, JACK. TOO MANY SMOKE BOMBS.
WHAT A PITY, YOU LOST YOUR SIDEKICK, ACE.
I LIKED IT BETTER WHEN YOU WERE ALL PLAYING CARDS.
HEH HEH... MAYBE YOU CAN GO EASY ON ME?
*WHOSE* TURN IS IT TO CLEAN THE BATHROOM?
NINJA, *DISAPPEAR.*

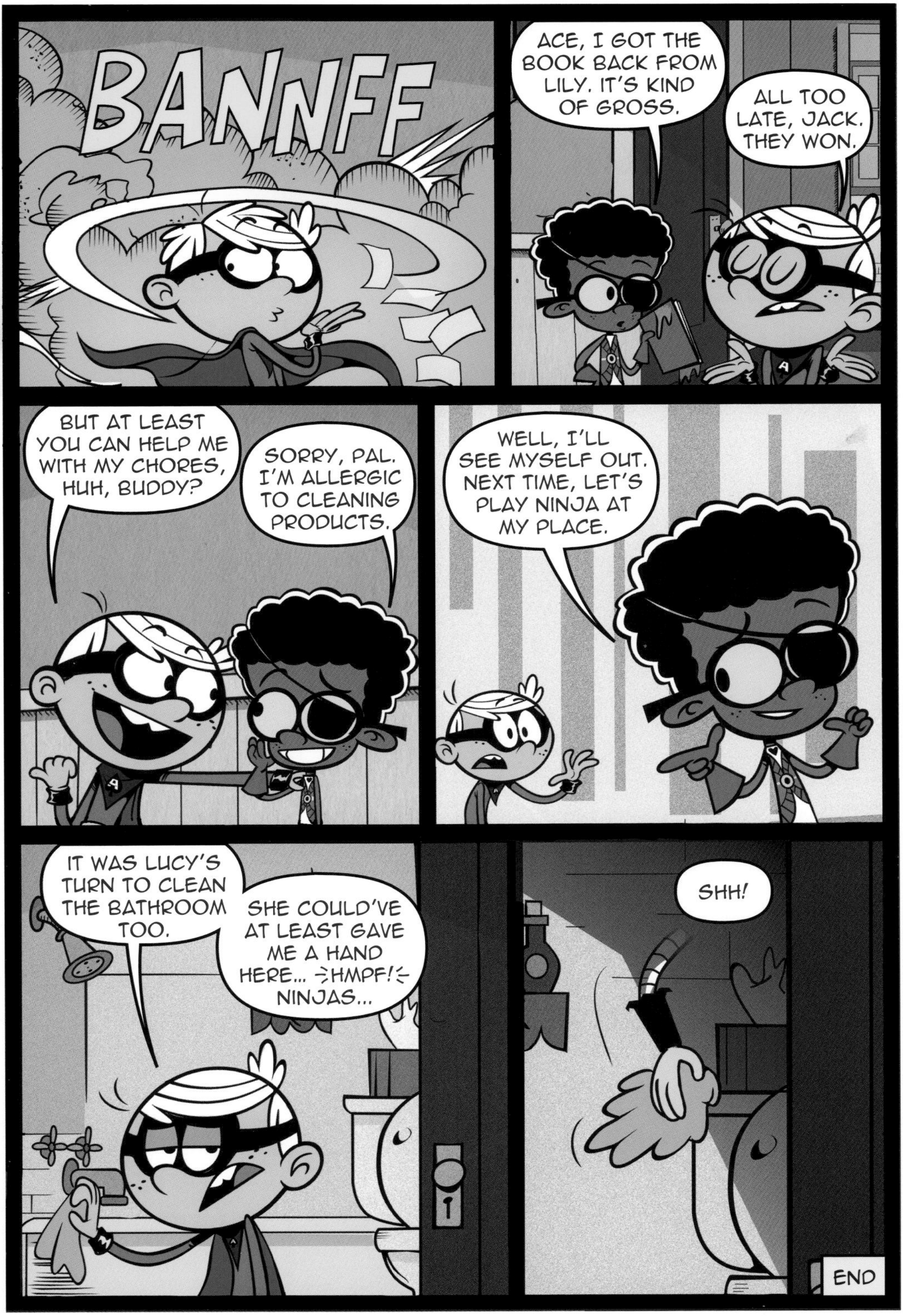
BANNFF
ACE, I GOT THE BOOK BACK FROM LILY. IT'S KIND OF GROSS.
ALL TOO LATE, JACK. THEY WON.
BUT AT LEAST YOU CAN HELP ME WITH MY CHORES, HUH, BUDDY?
SORRY, PAL. I'M ALLERGIC TO CLEANING PRODUCTS.
WELL, I'LL SEE MYSELF OUT. NEXT TIME, LET'S PLAY NINJA AT MY PLACE.
IT WAS LUCY'S TURN TO CLEAN THE BATHROOM TOO.
SHE COULD'VE AT LEAST GAVE ME A HAND HERE... HMPF! NINJAS...
SHH!
END

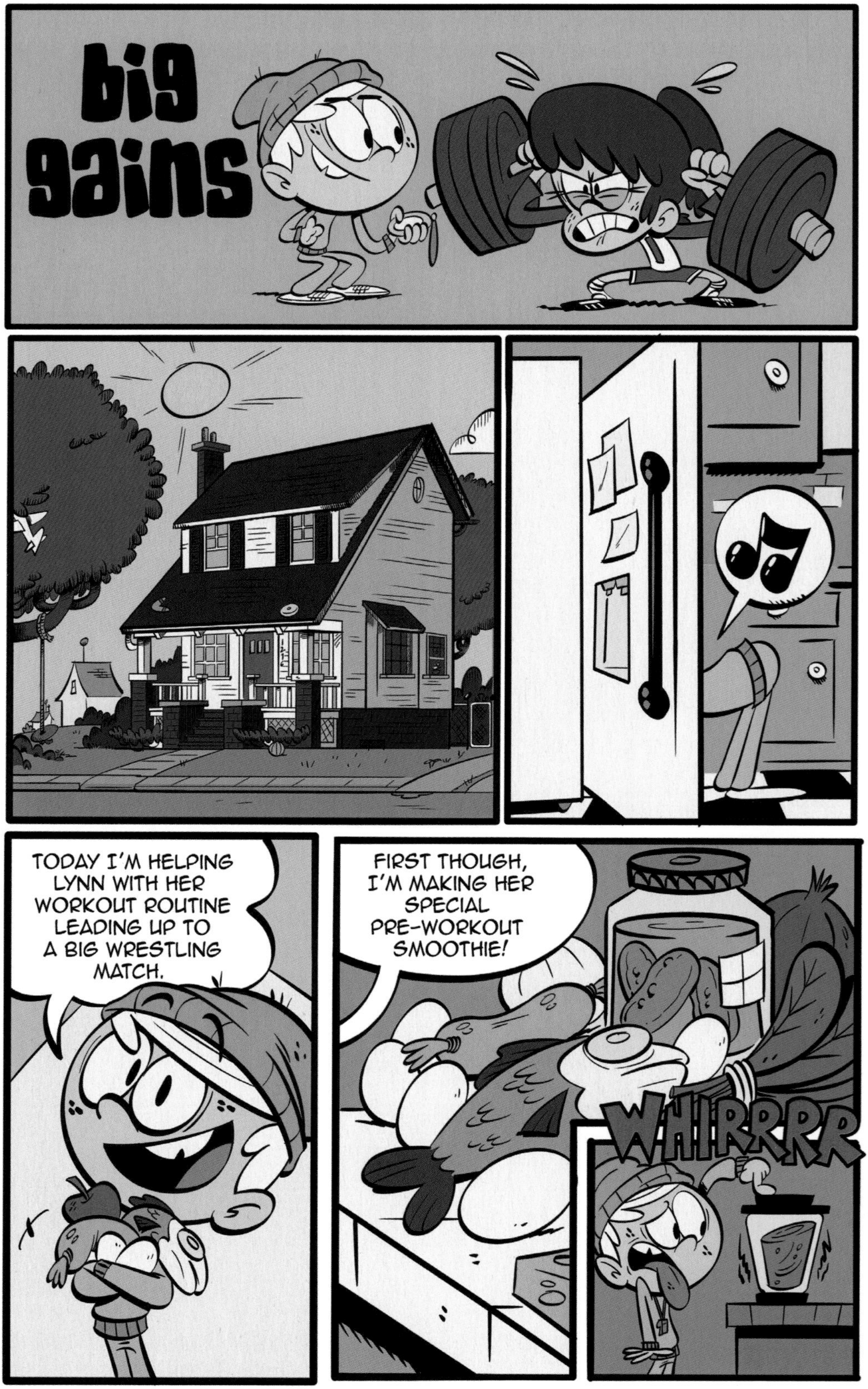
big gains
TODAY I'M HELPING LYNN WITH HER WORKOUT ROUTINE LEADING UP TO A BIG WRESTLING MATCH.
FIRST THOUGH, I'M MAKING HER SPECIAL PRE-WORKOUT SMOOTHIE!
WHIRRRR

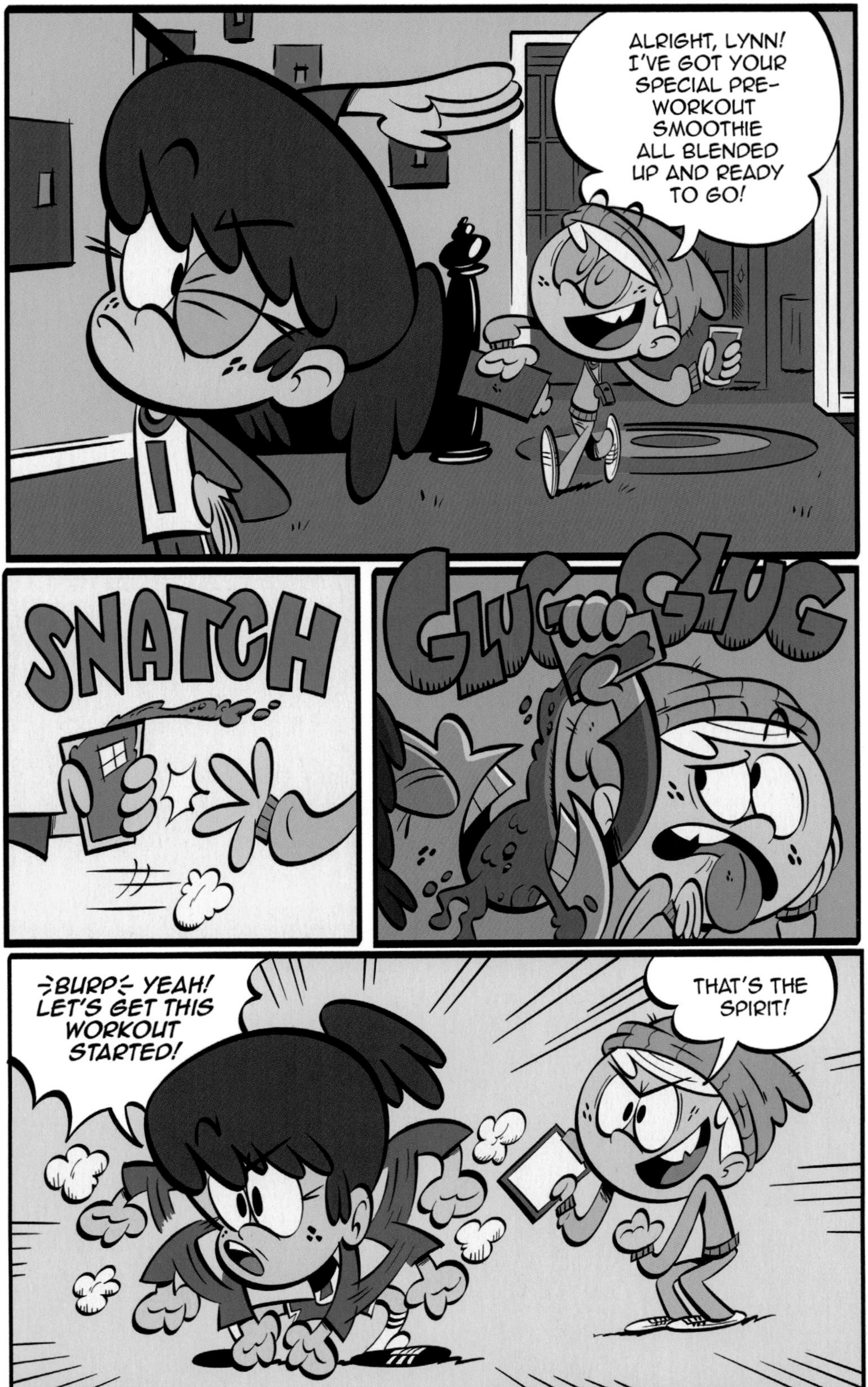
ALRIGHT, LYNN! I'VE GOT YOUR SPECIAL PRE-WORKOUT SMOOTHIE ALL BLENDED UP AND READY TO GO!
SNATCH
GLUG... GLUG
=BURP= YEAH! LET'S GET THIS WORKOUT STARTED!
THAT'S THE SPIRIT!

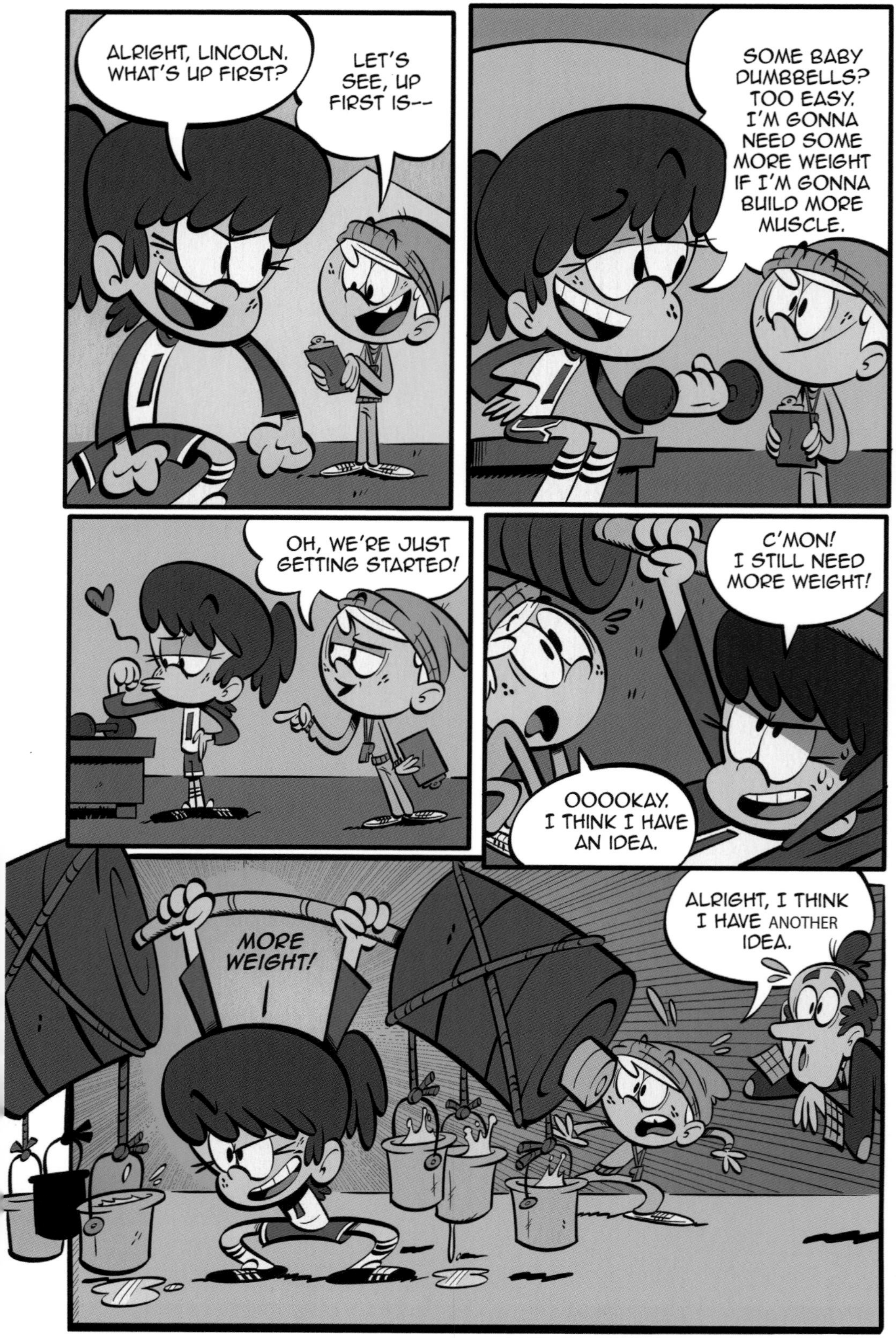
ALRIGHT, LINCOLN. WHAT'S UP FIRST?
LET'S SEE, UP FIRST IS--
SOME BABY DUMBBELLS? TOO EASY. I'M GONNA NEED SOME MORE WEIGHT IF I'M GONNA BUILD MORE MUSCLE.
OH, WE'RE JUST GETTING STARTED!
C'MON! I STILL NEED MORE WEIGHT!
OOOOKAY. I THINK I HAVE AN IDEA.
MORE WEIGHT!
ALRIGHT, I THINK I HAVE ANOTHER IDEA.

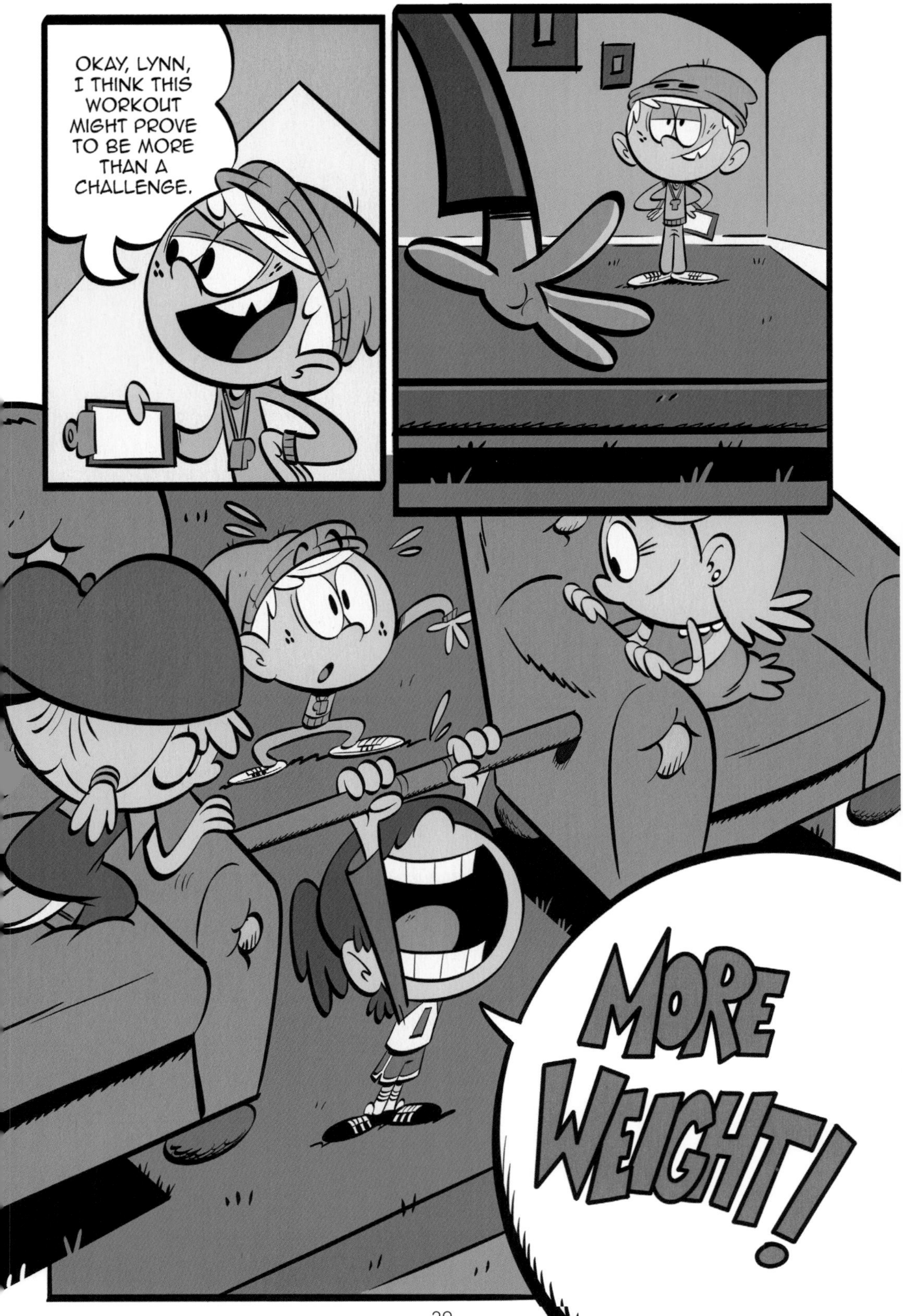
OKAY, LYNN, I THINK THIS WORKOUT MIGHT PROVE TO BE MORE THAN A CHALLENGE.
MORE WEIGHT!

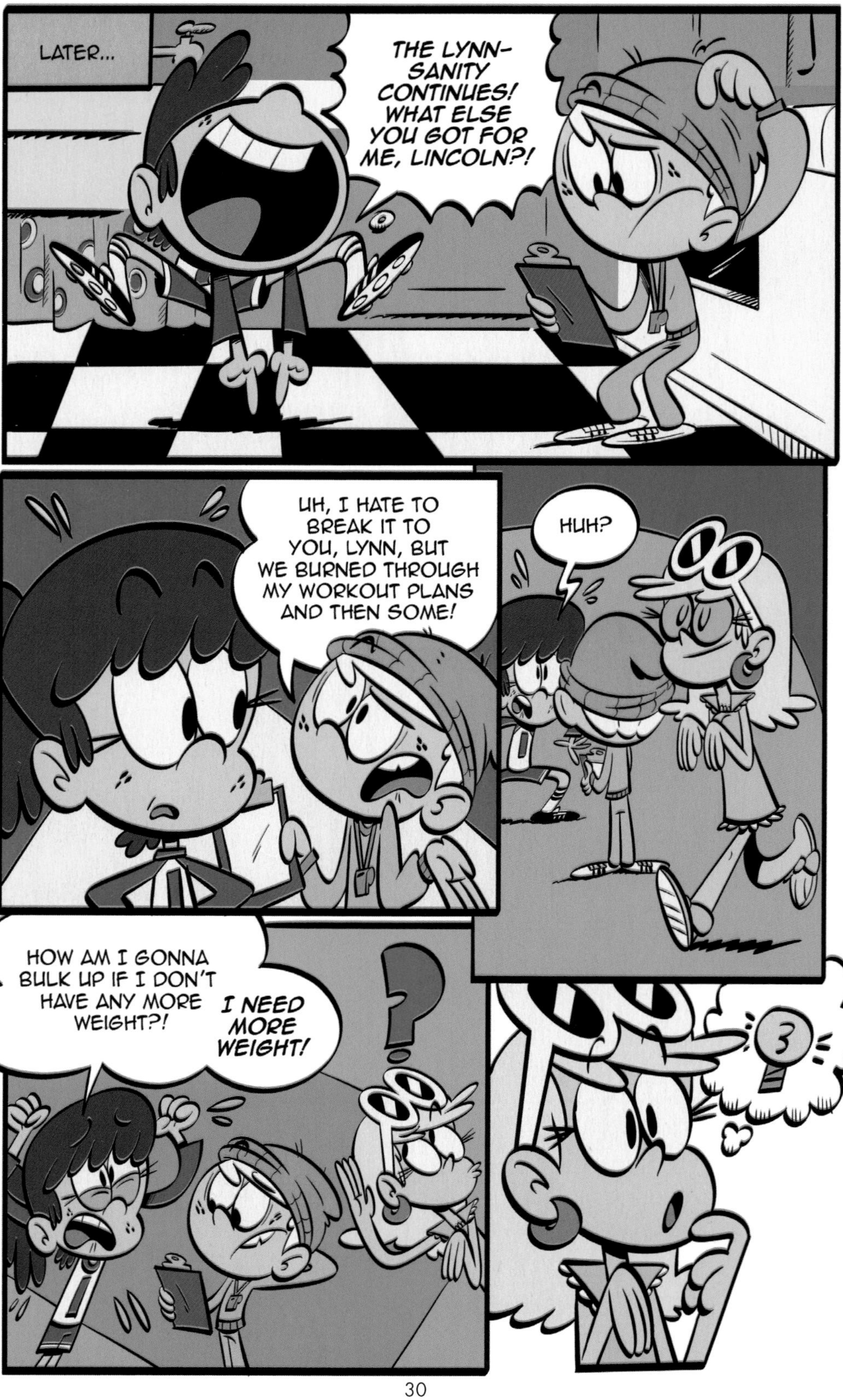
LATER...
THE LYNN-SANITY CONTINUES! WHAT ELSE YOU GOT FOR ME, LINCOLN?!
UH, I HATE TO BREAK IT TO YOU, LYNN, BUT WE BURNED THROUGH MY WORKOUT PLANS AND THEN SOME!
HUH?
HOW AM I GONNA BULK UP IF I DON'T HAVE ANY MORE WEIGHT?!
I NEED MORE WEIGHT!
3

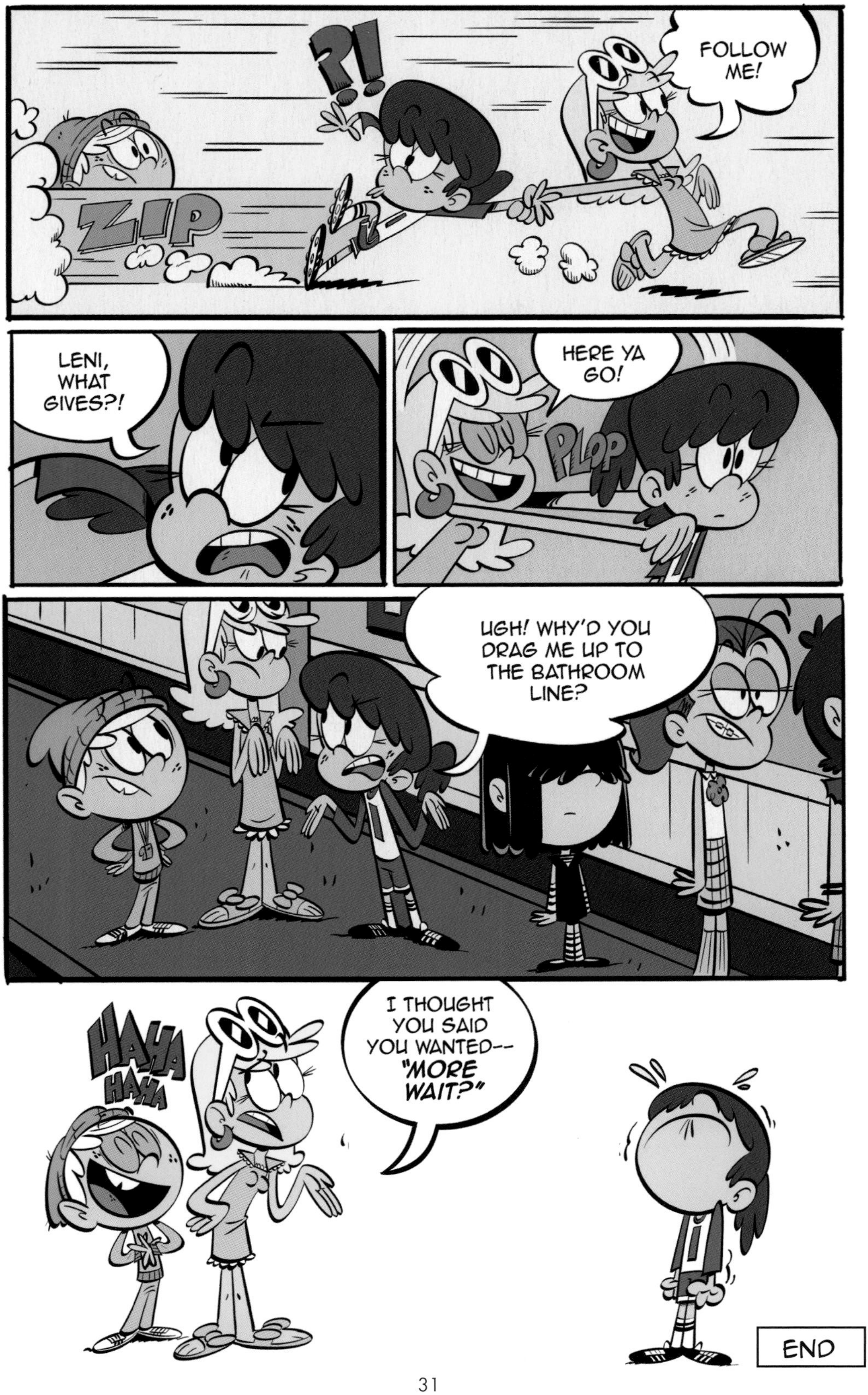
?!
FOLLOW ME!
ZIP
LENI, WHAT GIVES?!
HERE YA GO!
PLOP
UGH! WHY'D YOU DRAG ME UP TO THE BATHROOM LINE?
HAHA HAHA
I THOUGHT YOU SAID YOU WANTED-- "MORE WAIT?"
END

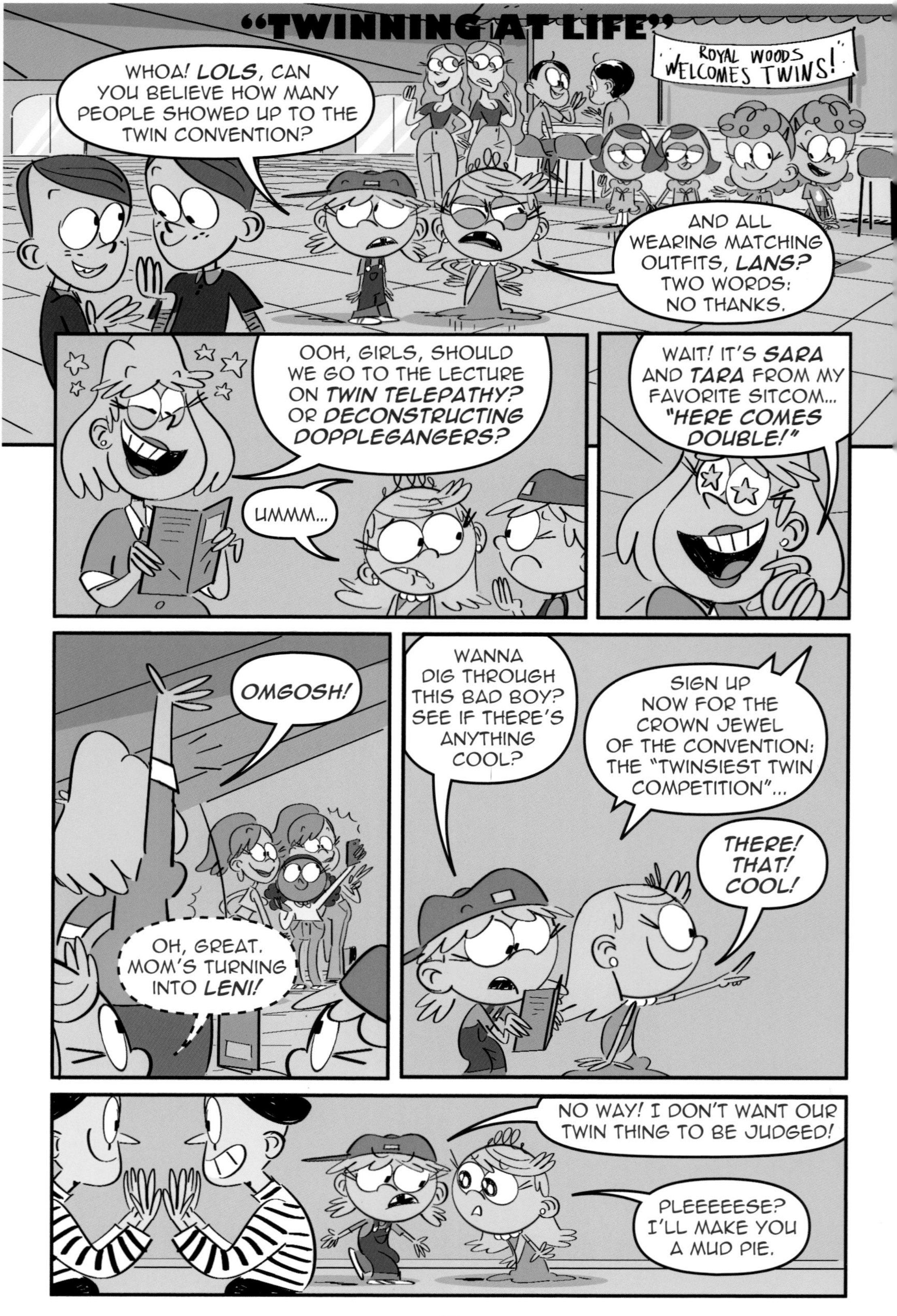
"TWINNING AT LIFE"
ROYAL WOODS WELCOMES TWINS!
WHOA! LOLS, CAN YOU BELIEVE HOW MANY PEOPLE SHOWED UP TO THE TWIN CONVENTION?
AND ALL WEARING MATCHING OUTFITS, LANS? TWO WORDS: NO THANKS.
OOH, GIRLS, SHOULD WE GO TO THE LECTURE ON TWIN TELEPATHY? OR DECONSTRUCTING DOPPLEGANGERS?
UMMM...
WAIT! IT'S SARA AND TARA FROM MY FAVORITE SITCOM... "HERE COMES DOUBLE!"
OMGOSH!
OH, GREAT. MOM'S TURNING INTO LENI!
WANNA DIG THROUGH THIS BAD BOY? SEE IF THERE'S ANYTHING COOL?
SIGN UP NOW FOR THE CROWN JEWEL OF THE CONVENTION: THE "TWINSIEST TWIN COMPETITION"...
THERE! THAT! COOL!
NO WAY! I DON'T WANT OUR TWIN THING TO BE JUDGED!
PLEEEEESE? I'LL MAKE YOU A MUD PIE.

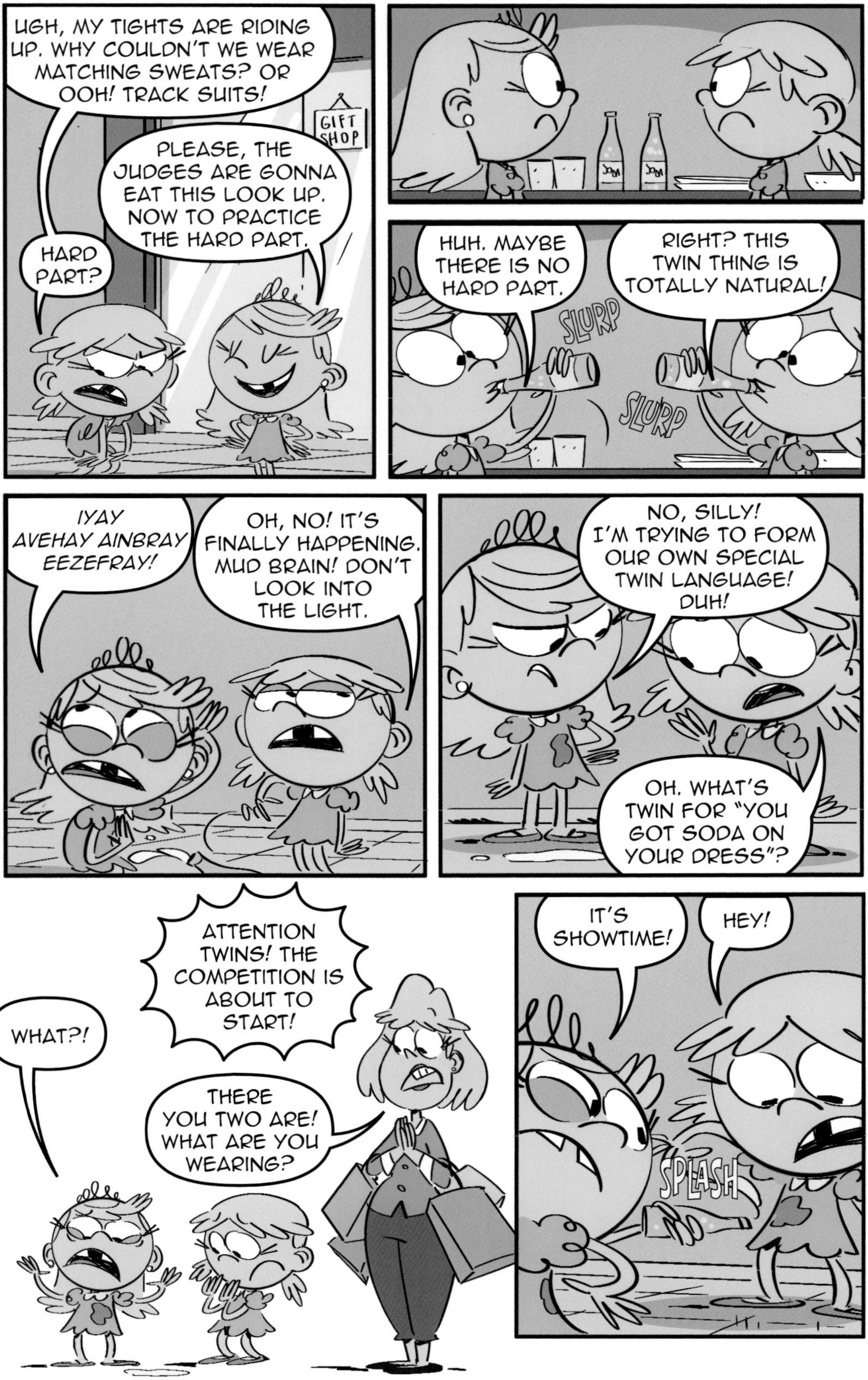
UGH, MY TIGHTS ARE RIDING UP. WHY COULDN'T WE WEAR MATCHING SWEATS? OR OOH! TRACK SUITS!
GIFT SHOP
PLEASE, THE JUDGES ARE GONNA EAT THIS LOOK UP. NOW TO PRACTICE THE HARD PART.
HARD PART?
HUH. MAYBE THERE IS NO HARD PART.
RIGHT? THIS TWIN THING IS TOTALLY NATURAL!
SLURP
SLURP
IYAY AVEHAY AINBRAY EEZEFRAY!
OH, NO! IT'S FINALLY HAPPENING. MUD BRAIN! DON'T LOOK INTO THE LIGHT.
NO, SILLY! I'M TRYING TO FORM OUR OWN SPECIAL TWIN LANGUAGE! DUH!
OH. WHAT'S TWIN FOR "YOU GOT SODA ON YOUR DRESS"?
ATTENTION TWINS! THE COMPETITION IS ABOUT TO START!
WHAT?!
THERE YOU TWO ARE! WHAT ARE YOU WEARING?
IT'S SHOWTIME!
HEY!
SPLASH

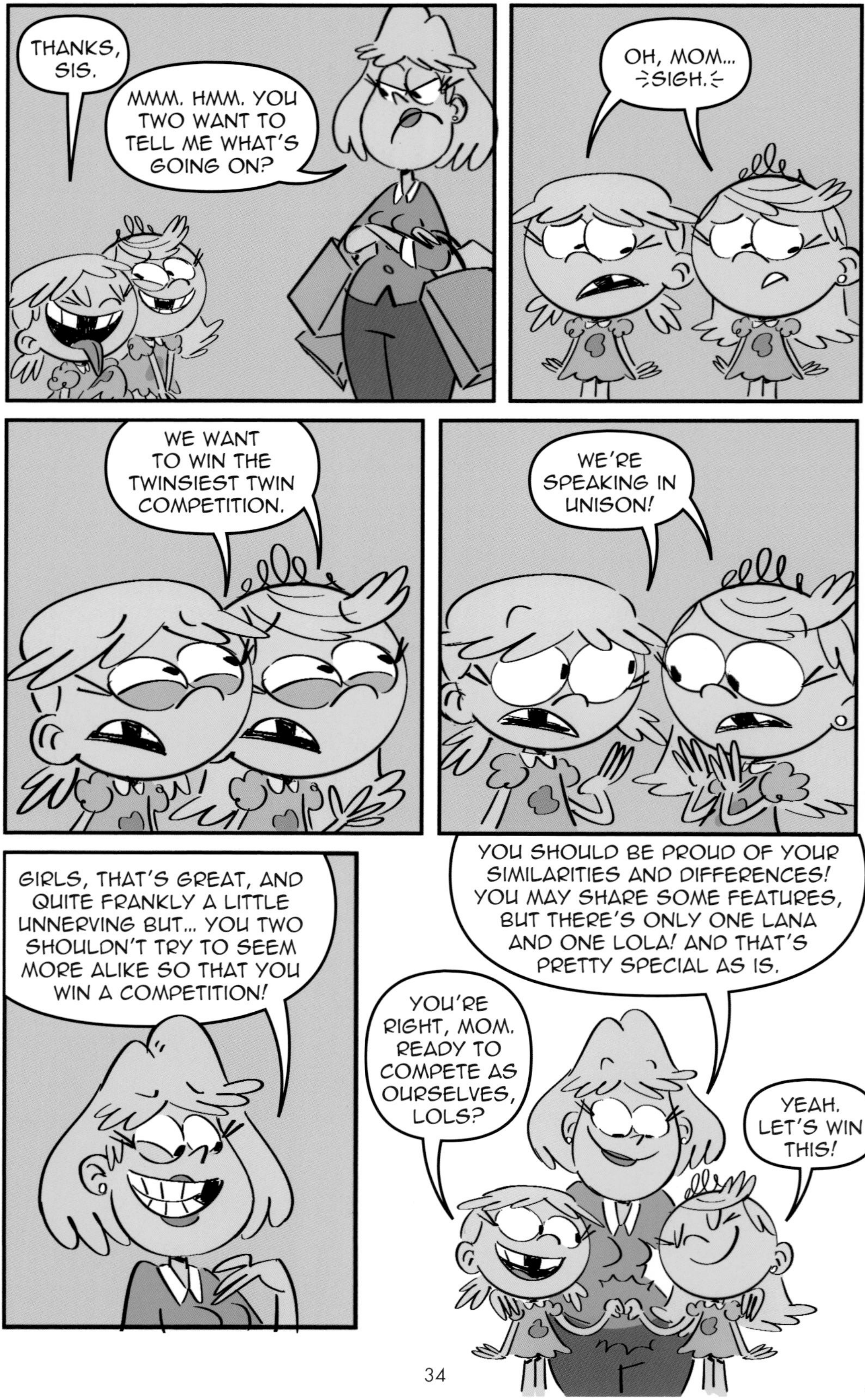
THANKS, SIS.
MMM. HMM. YOU TWO WANT TO TELL ME WHAT'S GOING ON?
OH, MOM... SIGH.
WE WANT TO WIN THE TWINSIEST TWIN COMPETITION.
WE'RE SPEAKING IN UNISON!
GIRLS, THAT'S GREAT, AND QUITE FRANKLY A LITTLE UNNERVING BUT... YOU TWO SHOULDN'T TRY TO SEEM MORE ALIKE SO THAT YOU WIN A COMPETITION!
YOU SHOULD BE PROUD OF YOUR SIMILARITIES AND DIFFERENCES! YOU MAY SHARE SOME FEATURES, BUT THERE'S ONLY ONE LANA AND ONE LOLA! AND THAT'S PRETTY SPECIAL AS IS.
YOU'RE RIGHT, MOM. READY TO COMPETE AS OURSELVES, LOLS?
YEAH. LET'S WIN THIS!

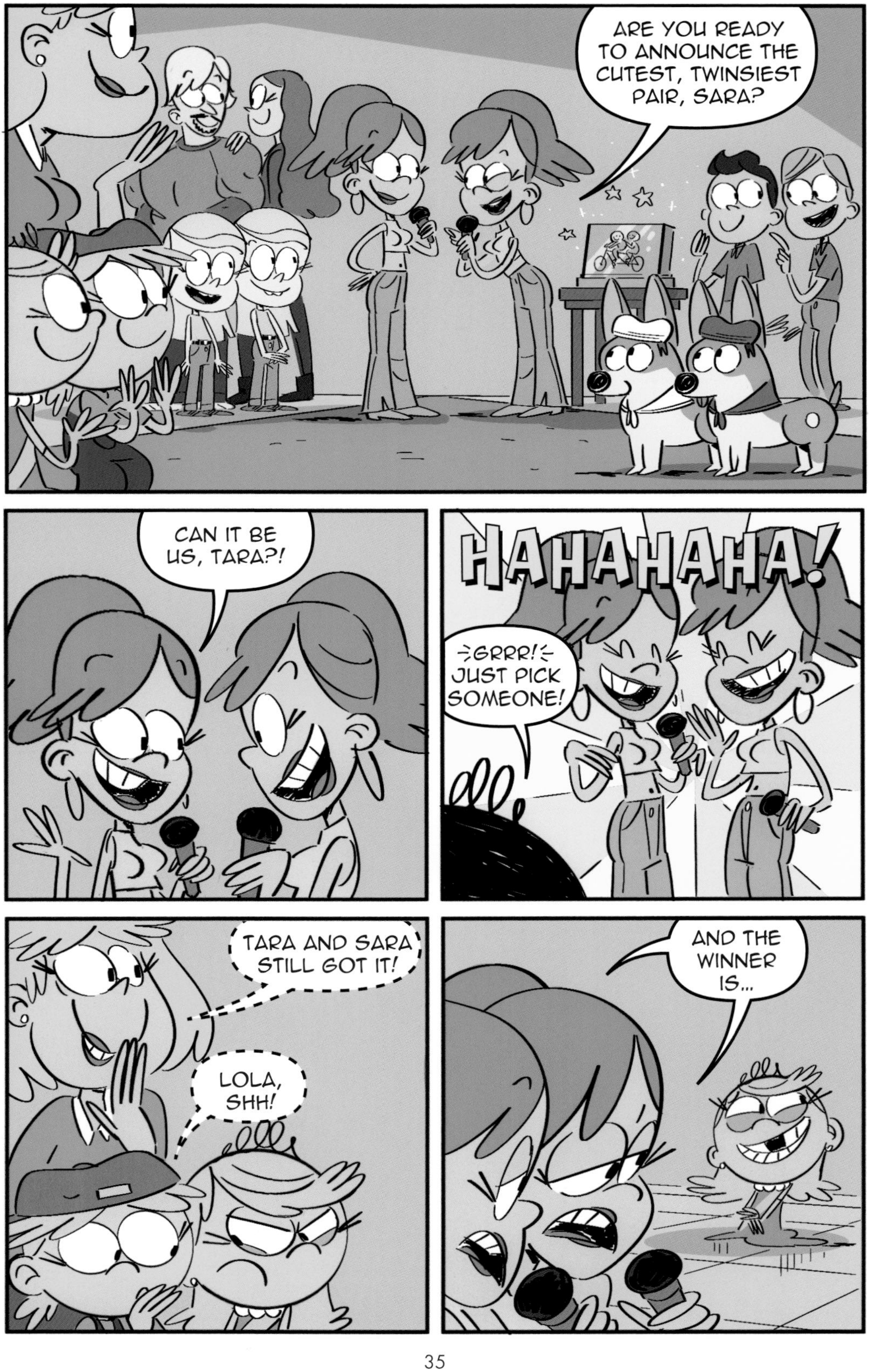

ARE YOU READY TO ANNOUNCE THE CUTEST, TWINSIEST PAIR, SARA?
CAN IT BE US, TARA?!
HAHAHAHA!
GRRR! JUST PICK SOMEONE!
TARA AND SARA STILL GOT IT!
LOLA, SHH!
AND THE WINNER IS...

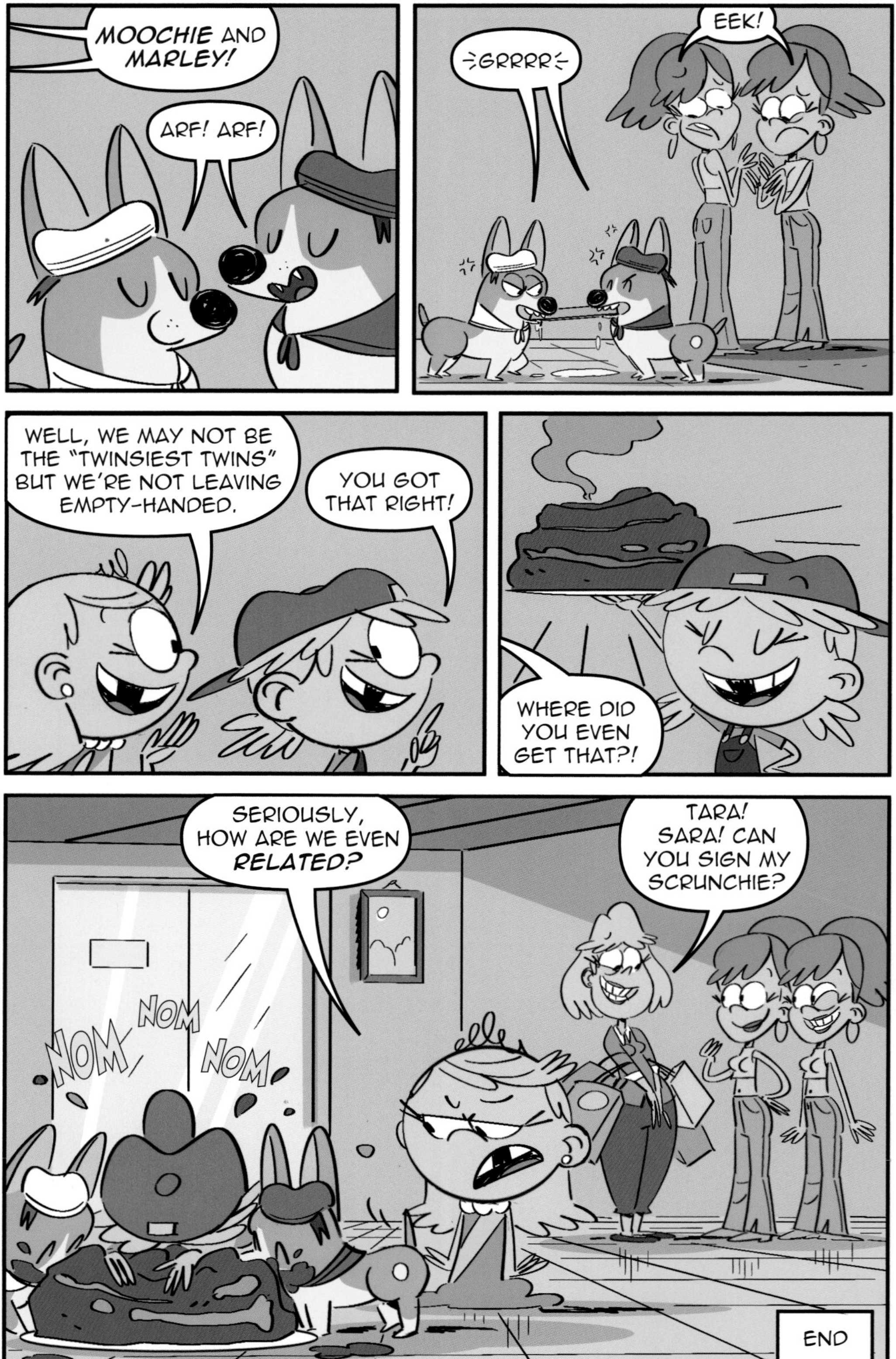
MOOCHIE AND MARLEY!
ARF! ARF!
GRRRR
EEK!
WELL, WE MAY NOT BE THE "TWINSIEST TWINS" BUT WE'RE NOT LEAVING EMPTY-HANDED.
YOU GOT THAT RIGHT!
WHERE DID YOU EVEN GET THAT?!
SERIOUSLY, HOW ARE WE EVEN RELATED?
TARA! SARA! CAN YOU SIGN MY SCRUNCHIE?
NOM
NOM
NOM
END

# "MODEL BEHAVIOR"

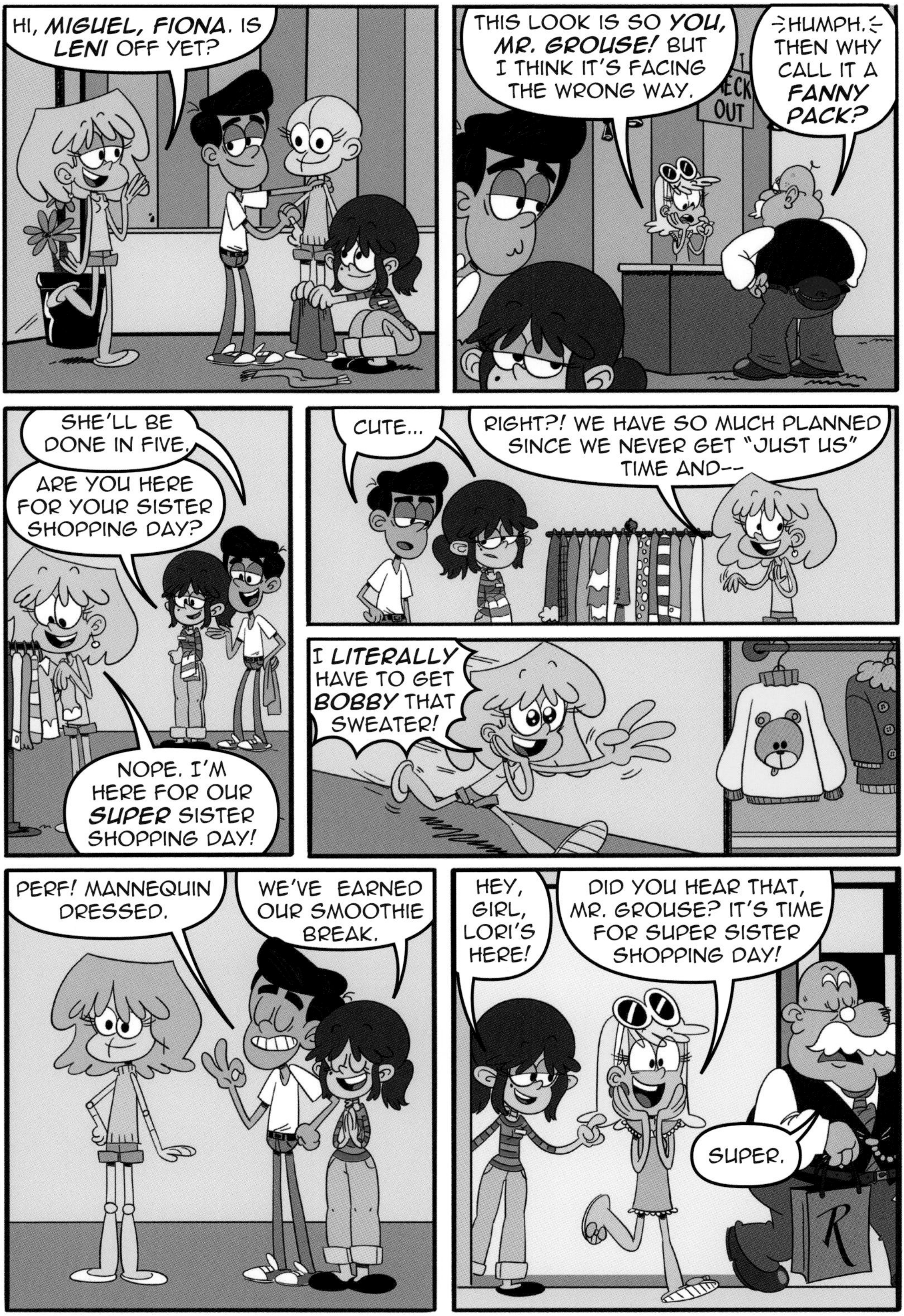

HI, MIGUEL, FIONA. IS LENI OFF YET?
THIS LOOK IS SO YOU, MR. GROUSE! BUT I THINK IT'S FACING THE WRONG WAY.
HUMPH. THEN WHY CALL IT A FANNY PACK?
CHECK OUT
SHE'LL BE DONE IN FIVE.
ARE YOU HERE FOR YOUR SISTER SHOPPING DAY?
NOPE. I'M HERE FOR OUR SUPER SISTER SHOPPING DAY!
CUTE...
RIGHT?! WE HAVE SO MUCH PLANNED SINCE WE NEVER GET "JUST US" TIME AND--
I LITERALLY HAVE TO GET BOBBY THAT SWEATER!
PERF! MANNEQUIN DRESSED.
WE'VE EARNED OUR SMOOTHIE BREAK.
HEY, GIRL, LORI'S HERE!
DID YOU HEAR THAT, MR. GROUSE? IT'S TIME FOR SUPER SISTER SHOPPING DAY!
SUPER.
R

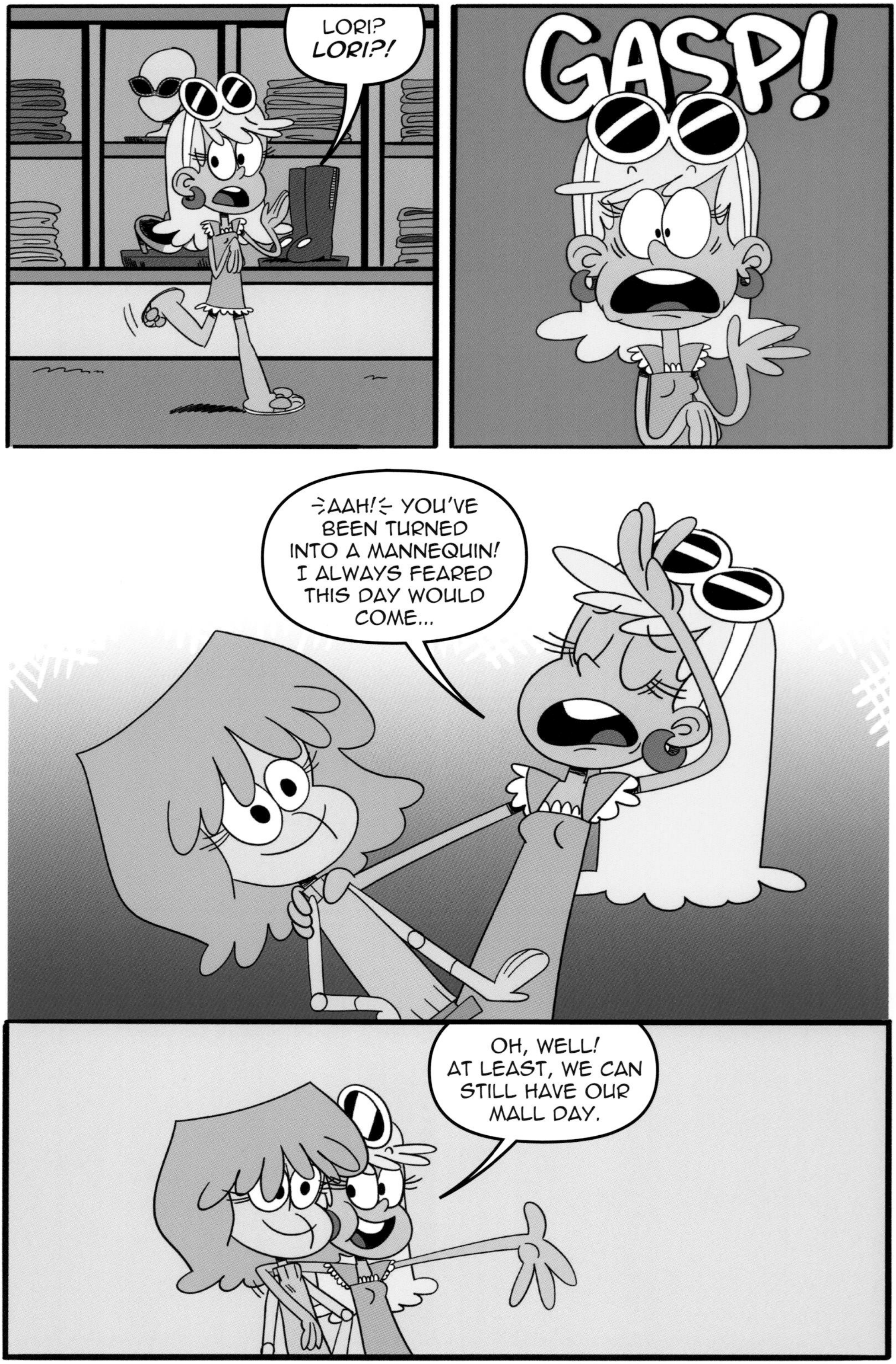
LORI? LORI?!
GASP!
AAH! YOU'VE BEEN TURNED INTO A MANNEQUIN! I ALWAYS FEARED THIS DAY WOULD COME...
OH, WELL! AT LEAST, WE CAN STILL HAVE OUR MALL DAY.

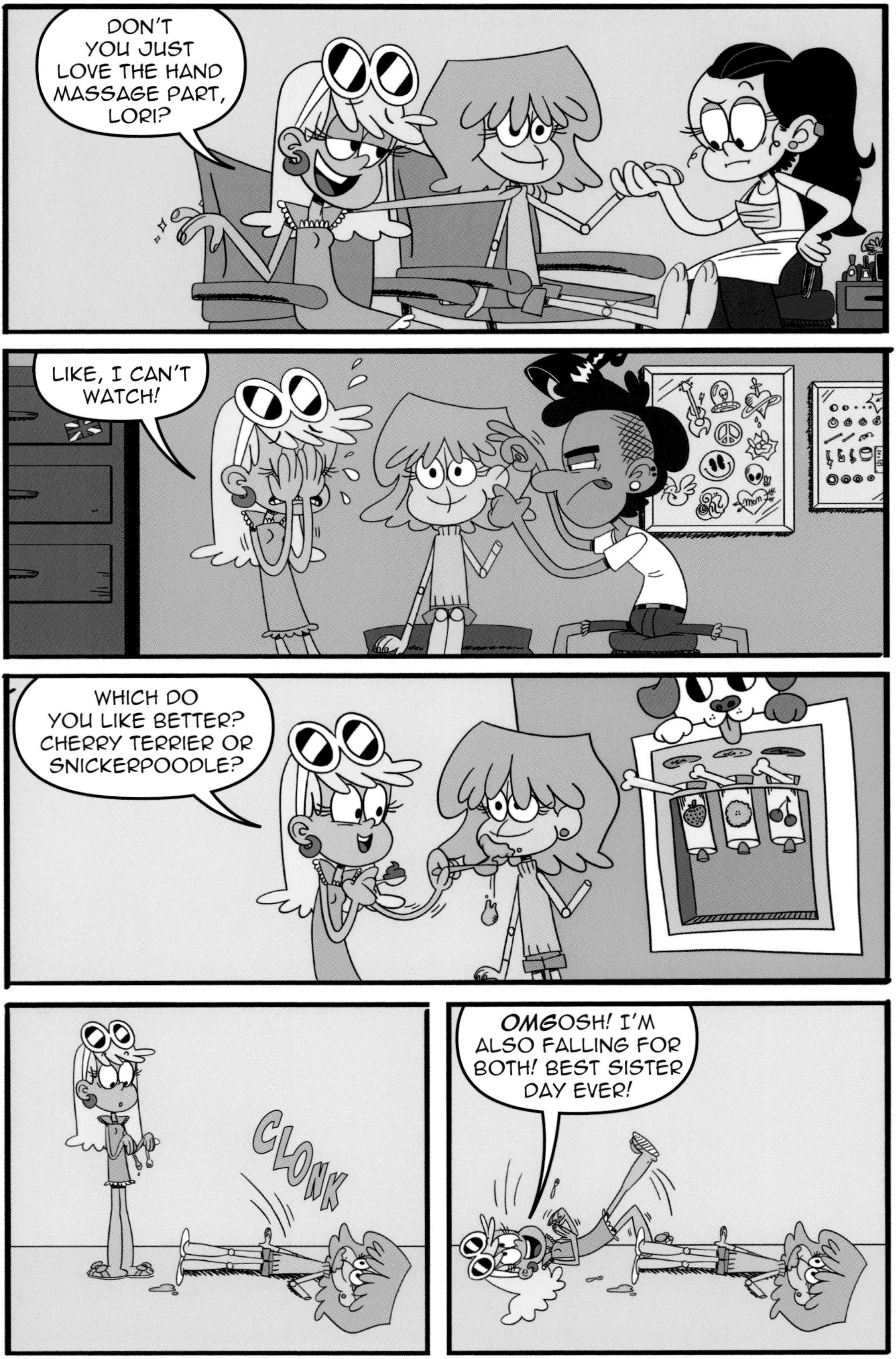
DON'T YOU JUST LOVE THE HAND MASSAGE PART, LORI?
LIKE, I CAN'T WATCH!
WHICH DO YOU LIKE BETTER? CHERRY TERRIER OR SNICKERPOODLE?
CLONK
OMGOSH! I'M ALSO FALLING FOR BOTH! BEST SISTER DAY EVER!

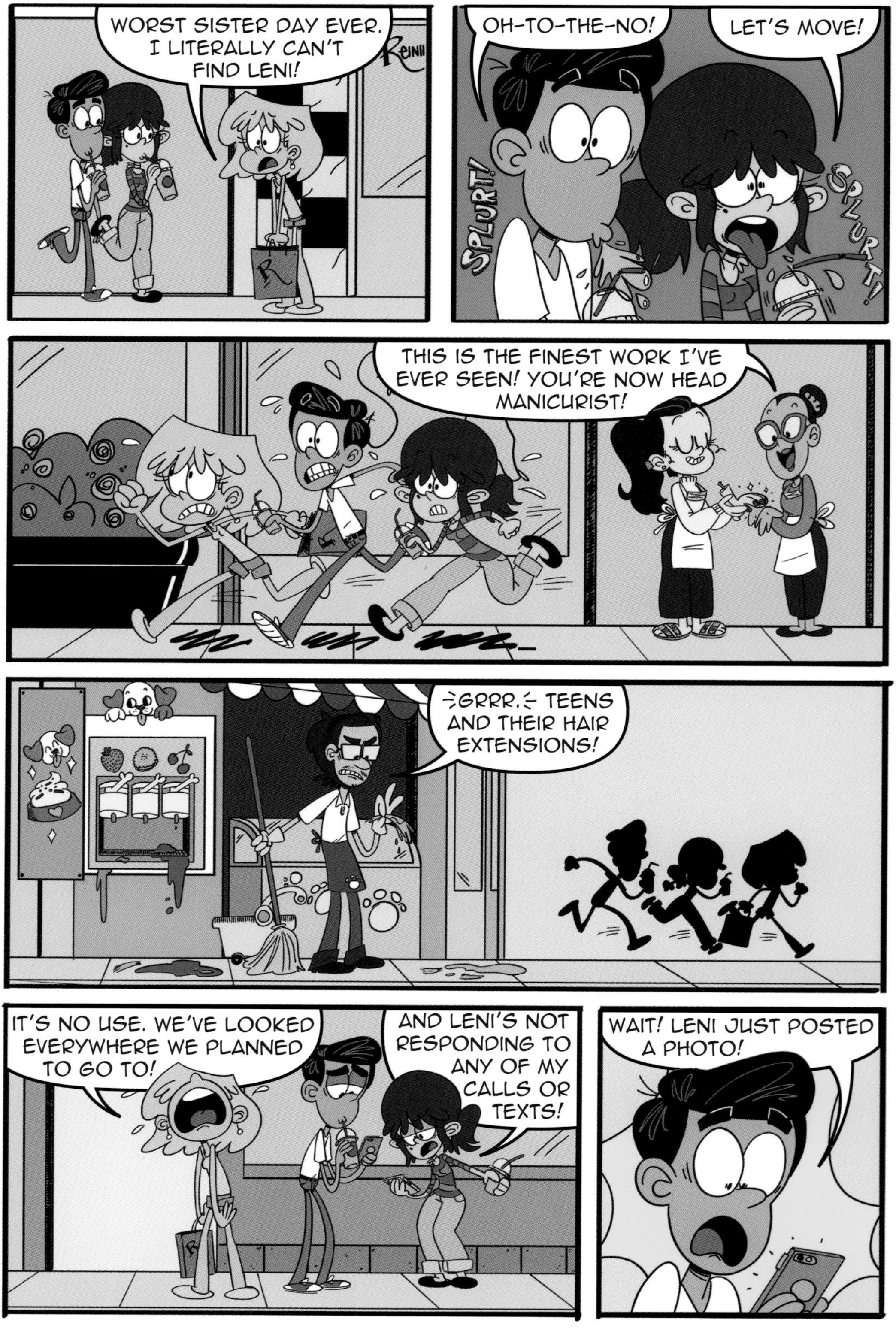
WORST SISTER DAY EVER. I LITERALLY CAN'T FIND LENI!
OH-TO-THE-NO!
LET'S MOVE!
SPLURT!
SPLURT!
THIS IS THE FINEST WORK I'VE EVER SEEN! YOU'RE NOW HEAD MANICURIST!
GRRR. TEENS AND THEIR HAIR EXTENSIONS!
IT'S NO USE. WE'VE LOOKED EVERYWHERE WE PLANNED TO GO TO!
AND LENI'S NOT RESPONDING TO ANY OF MY CALLS OR TEXTS!
WAIT! LENI JUST POSTED A PHOTO!

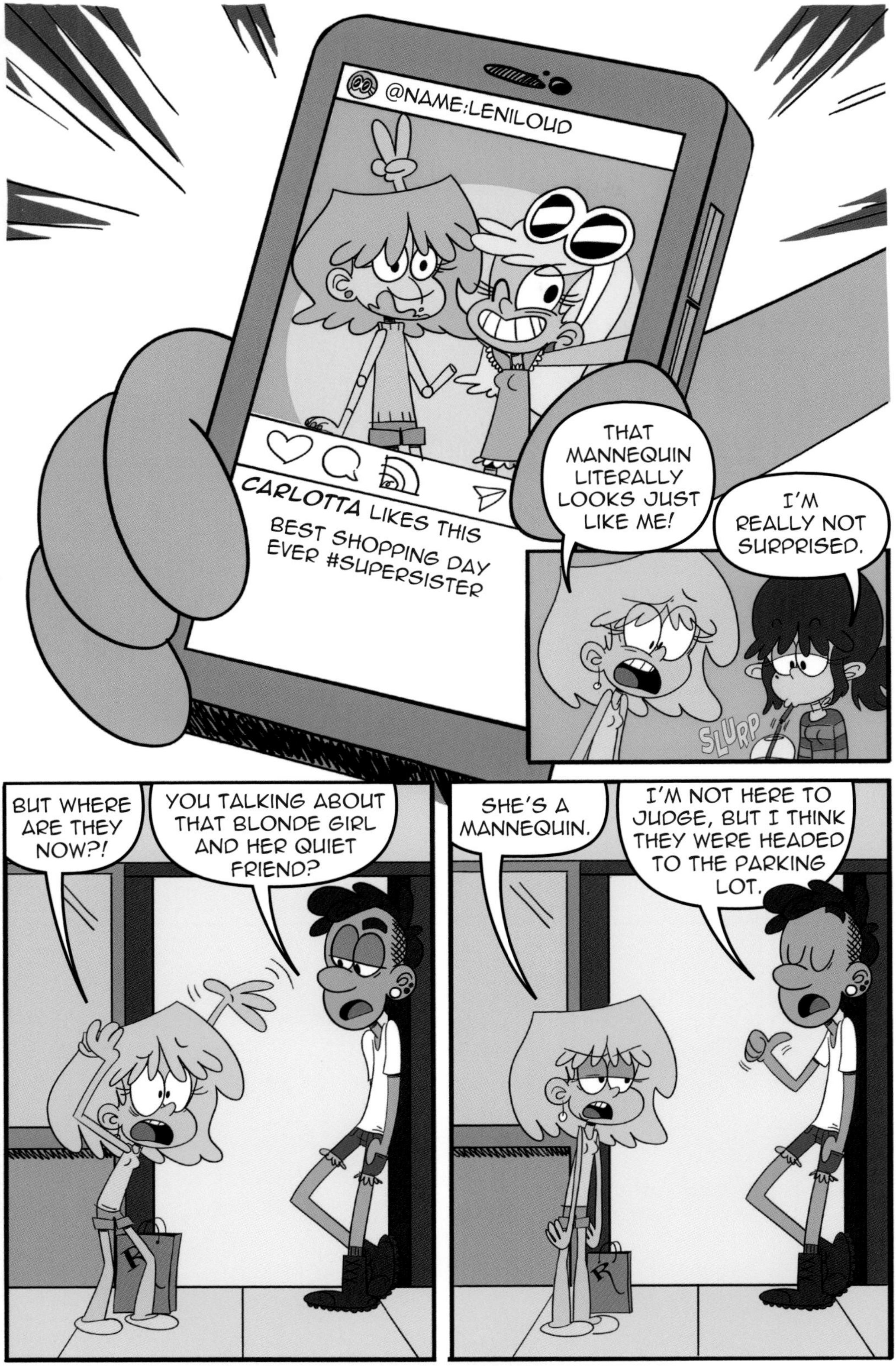
@NAME:LENILOUD
CARLOTTA LIKES THIS
BEST SHOPPING DAY EVER #SUPERSISTER
THAT MANNEQUIN LITERALLY LOOKS JUST LIKE ME!
I'M REALLY NOT SURPRISED.
SLURP
BUT WHERE ARE THEY NOW?!
YOU TALKING ABOUT THAT BLONDE GIRL AND HER QUIET FRIEND?
SHE'S A MANNEQUIN.
I'M NOT HERE TO JUDGE, BUT I THINK THEY WERE HEADED TO THE PARKING LOT.

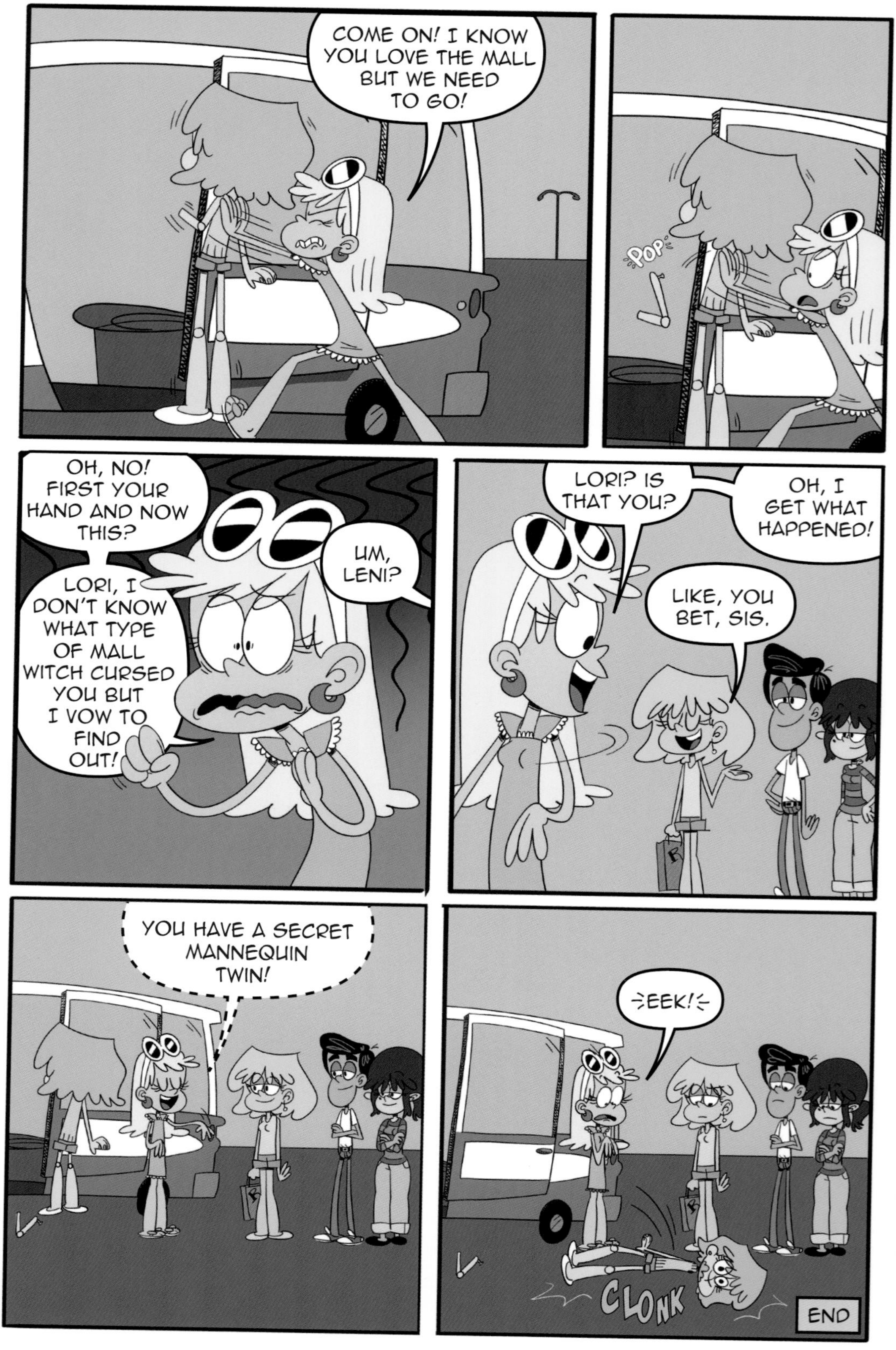
COME ON! I KNOW YOU LOVE THE MALL BUT WE NEED TO GO!
POP
OH, NO! FIRST YOUR HAND AND NOW THIS?
LORI, I DON'T KNOW WHAT TYPE OF MALL WITCH CURSED YOU BUT I VOW TO FIND OUT!
UM, LENI?
LORI? IS THAT YOU?
OH, I GET WHAT HAPPENED!
LIKE, YOU BET, SIS.
YOU HAVE A SECRET MANNEQUIN TWIN!
EEK!
CLONK
END

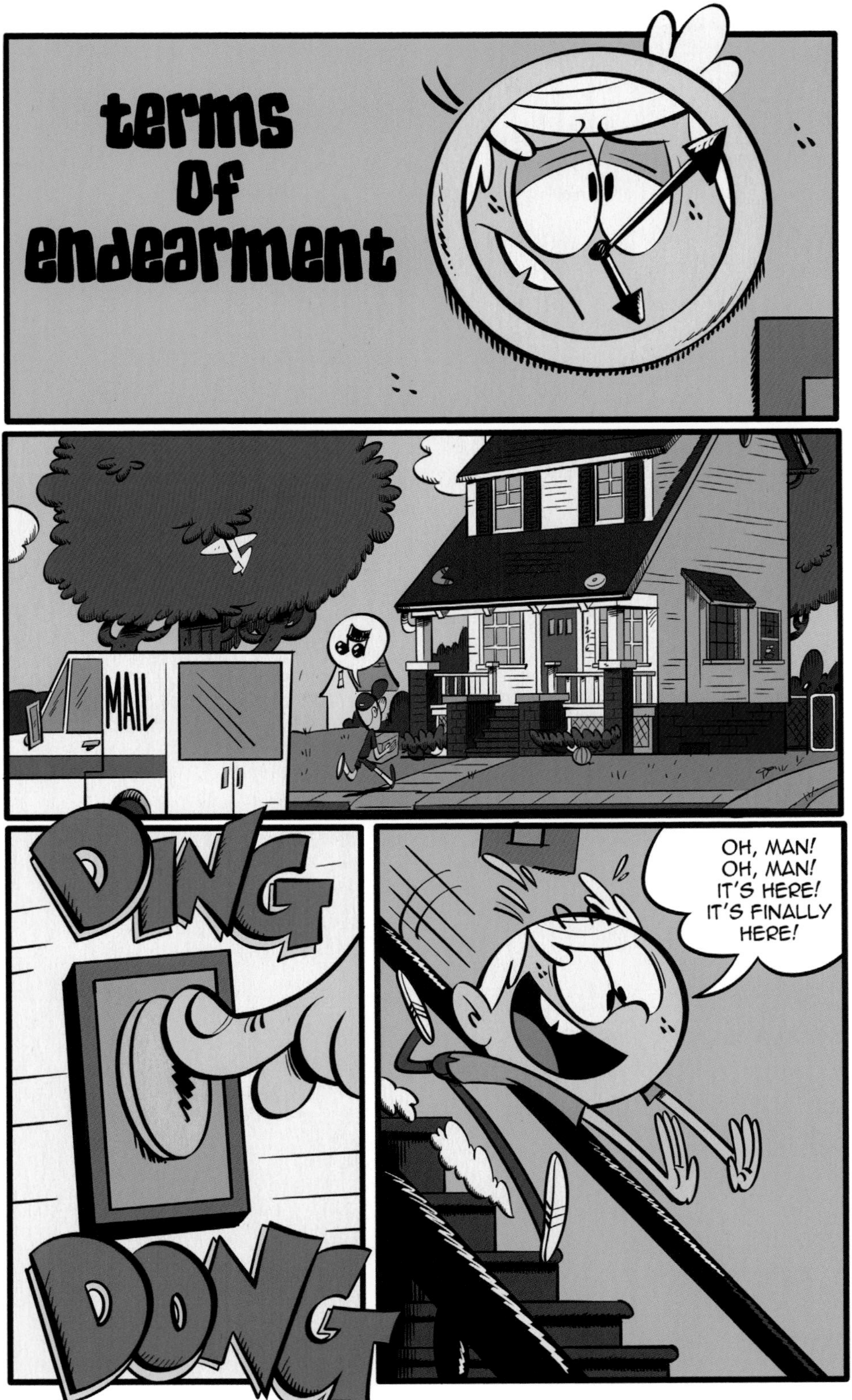
terms
of
endearment
MAIL
DING
DONG
OH, MAN!
OH, MAN!
IT'S HERE!
IT'S FINALLY
HERE!

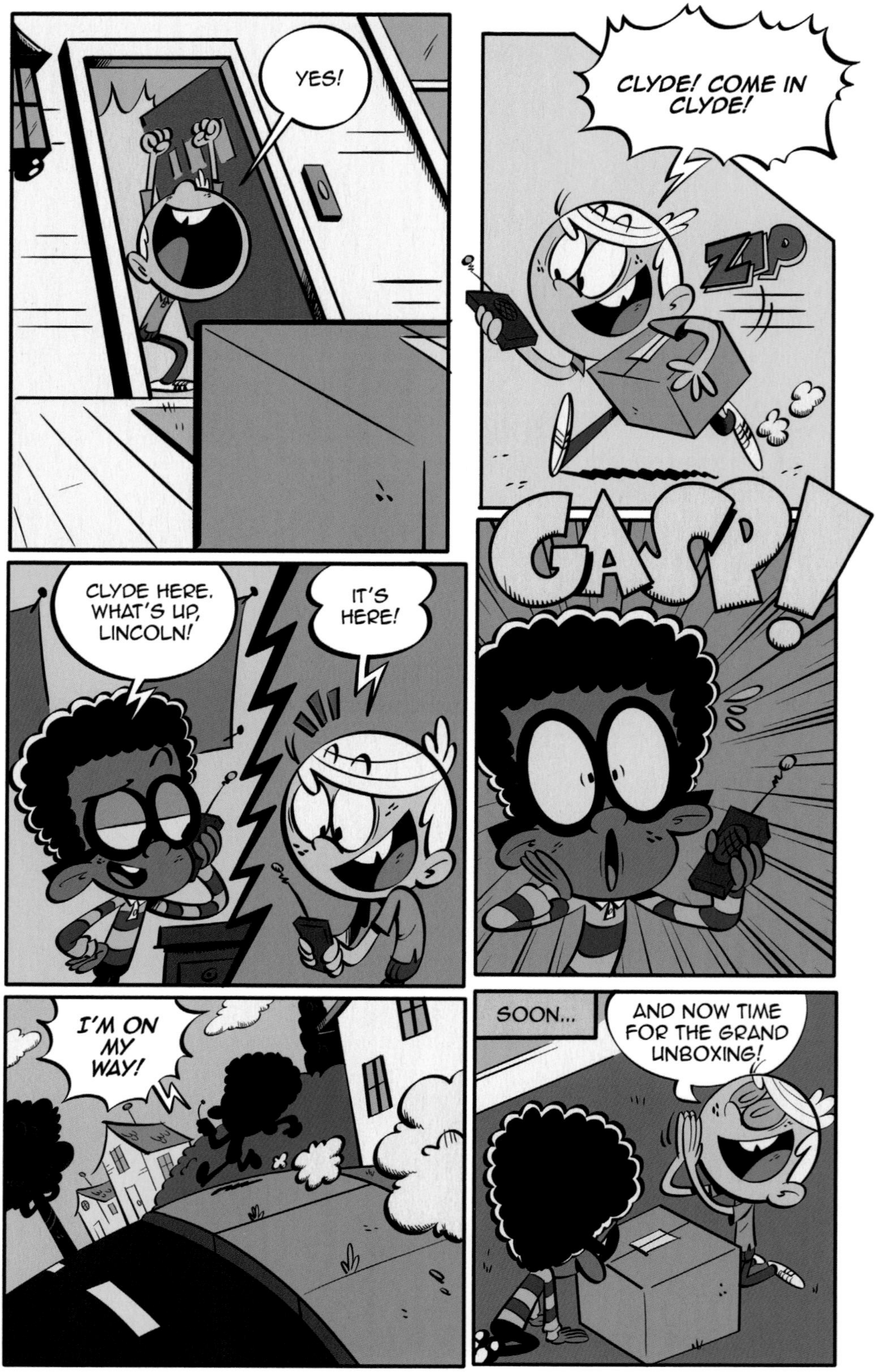
YES!
CLYDE! COME IN CLYDE!
ZIP
GASP!
CLYDE HERE. WHAT'S UP, LINCOLN!
IT'S HERE!
I'M ON MY WAY!
SOON...
AND NOW TIME FOR THE GRAND UNBOXING!

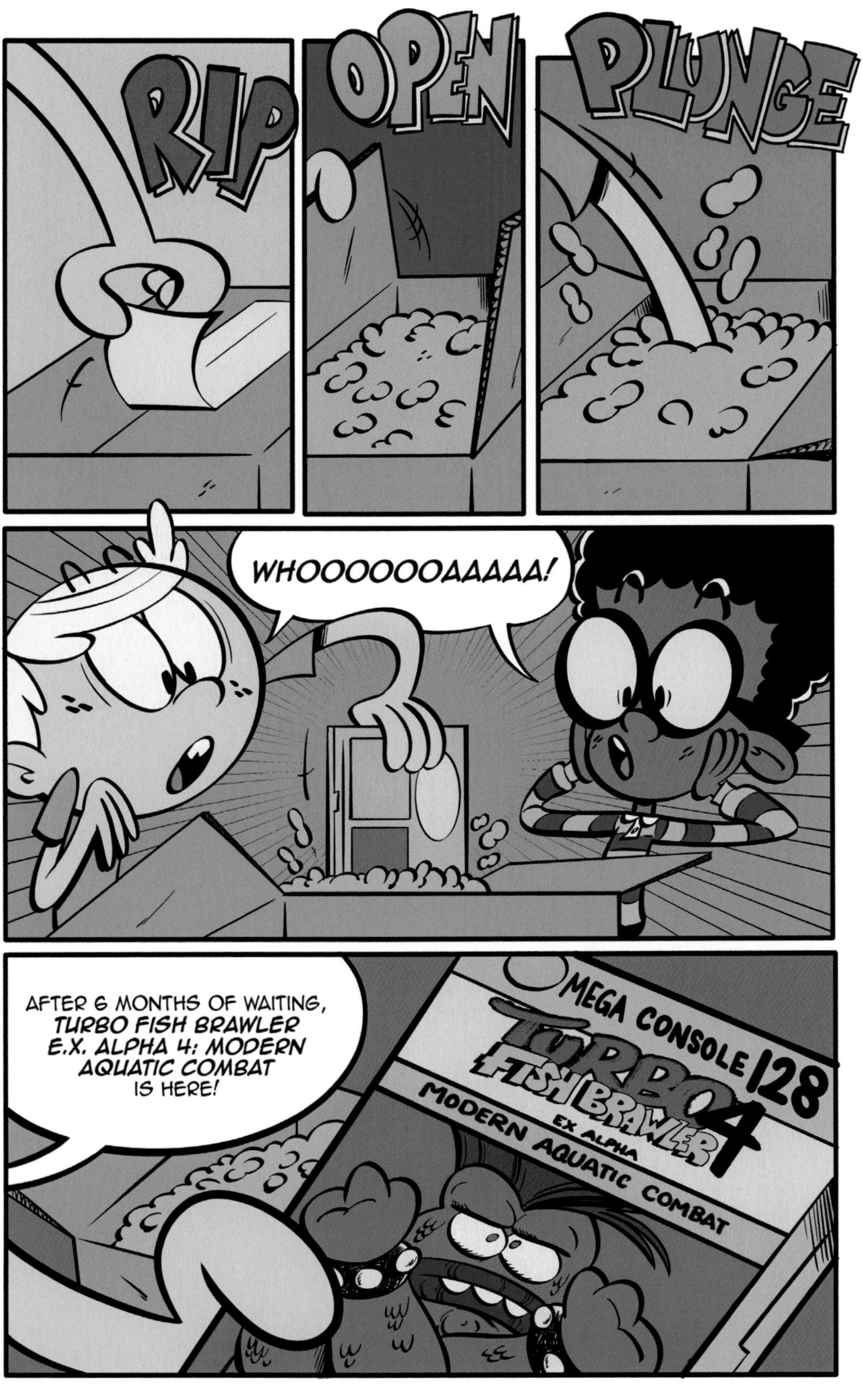

RIP
OPEN
PLUNGE
WHOOOOOOAAAAA!
AFTER 6 MONTHS OF WAITING, TURBO FISH BRAWLER E.X. ALPHA 4: MODERN AQUATIC COMBAT IS HERE!
MEGA CONSOLE 128
TURBO FISH BRAWLER EX ALPHA 4
MODERN AQUATIC COMBAT

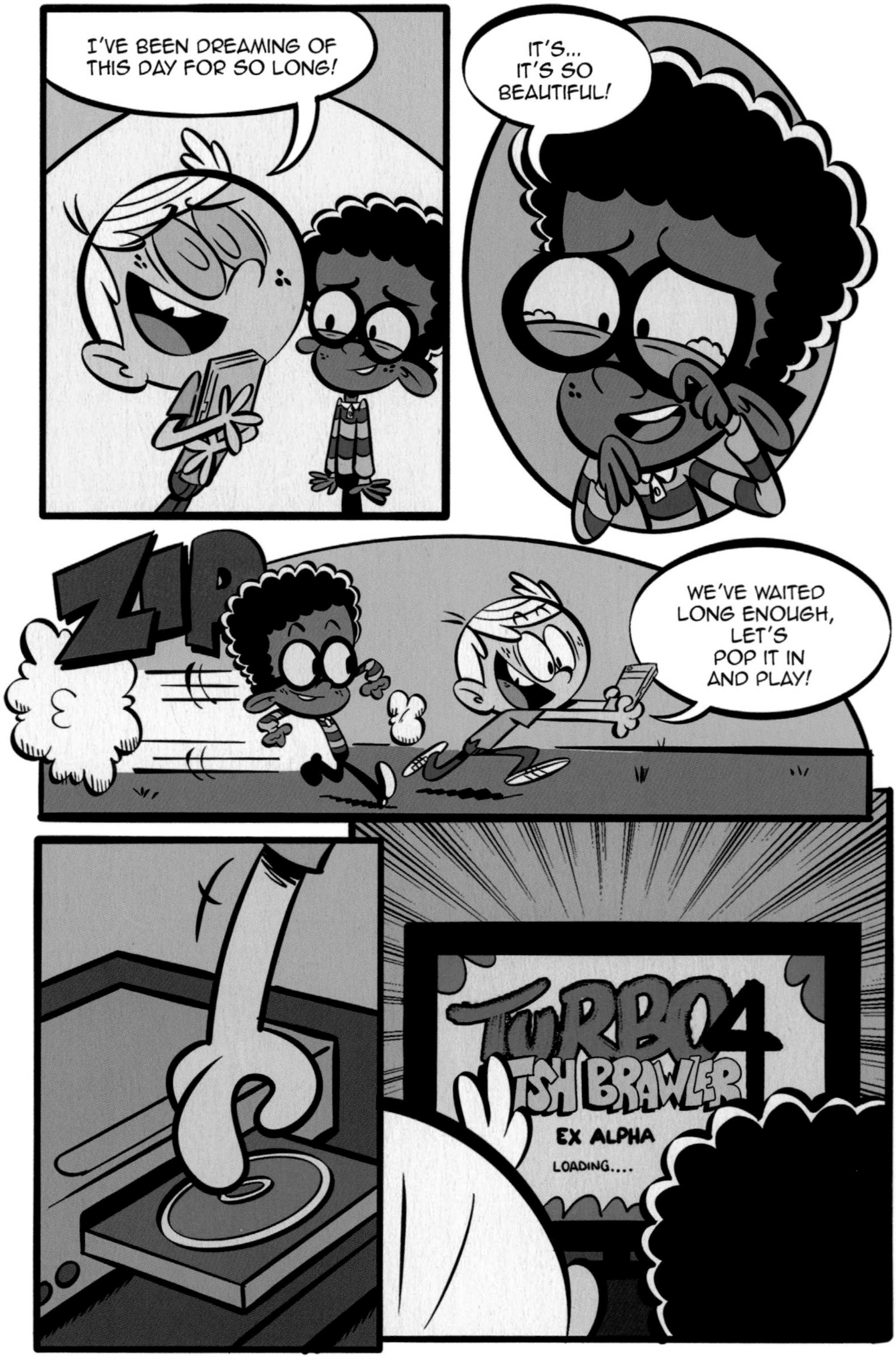
I'VE BEEN DREAMING OF THIS DAY FOR SO LONG!
IT'S... IT'S SO BEAUTIFUL!
ZIP
WE'VE WAITED LONG ENOUGH, LET'S POP IT IN AND PLAY!
TURBO 4
ISH BRAWLER
EX ALPHA
LOADING....

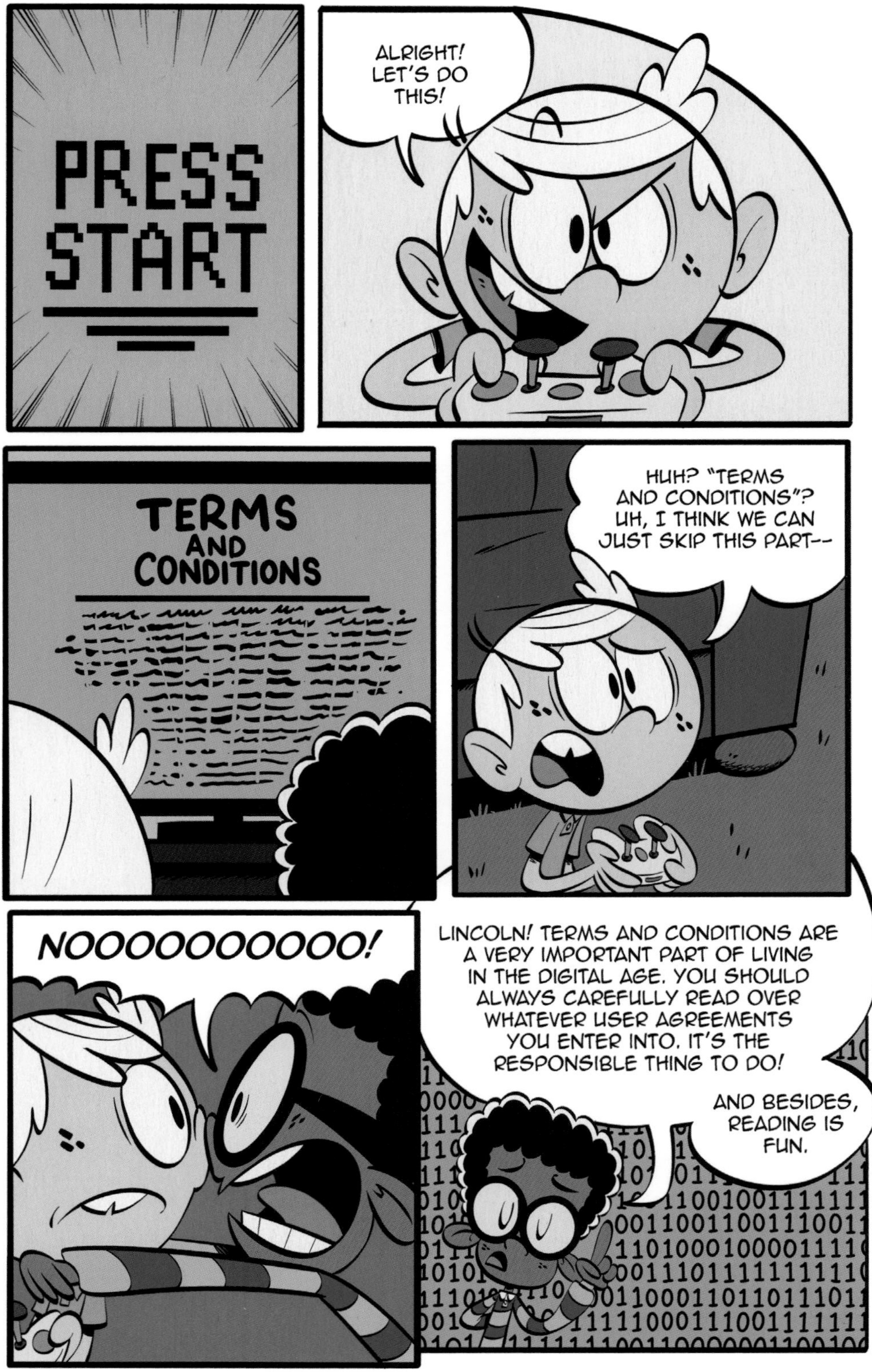
PRESS START
ALRIGHT! LET'S DO THIS!
TERMS AND CONDITIONS
HUH? "TERMS AND CONDITIONS"? UH, I THINK WE CAN JUST SKIP THIS PART--
NOOOOOOOOOO!
LINCOLN! TERMS AND CONDITIONS ARE A VERY IMPORTANT PART OF LIVING IN THE DIGITAL AGE. YOU SHOULD ALWAYS CAREFULLY READ OVER WHATEVER USER AGREEMENTS YOU ENTER INTO. IT'S THE RESPONSIBLE THING TO DO!
AND BESIDES, READING IS FUN.

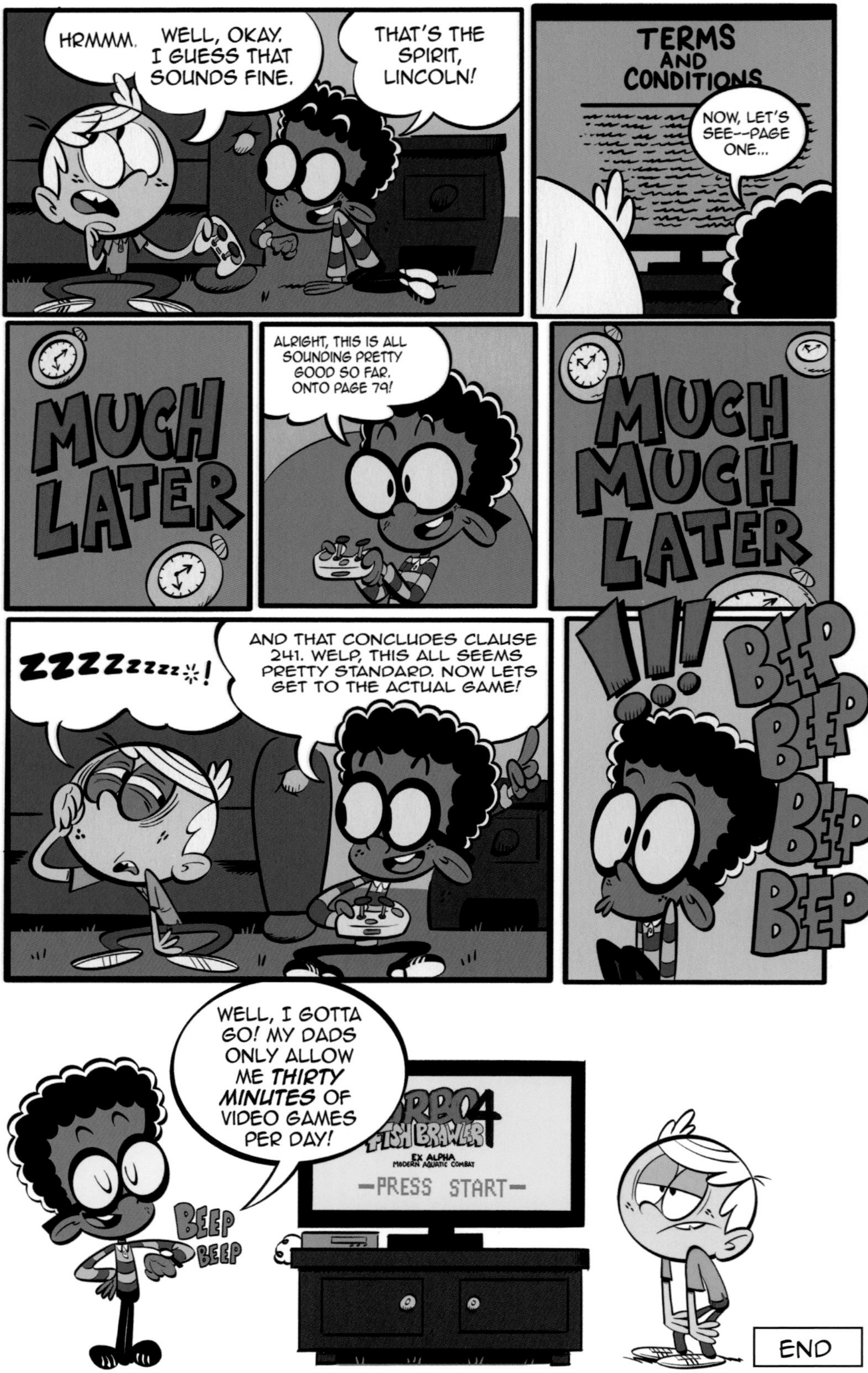
HRMMM.
WELL, OKAY. I GUESS THAT SOUNDS FINE.
THAT'S THE SPIRIT, LINCOLN!
TERMS AND CONDITIONS
NOW, LET'S SEE--PAGE ONE...
MUCH LATER
ALRIGHT, THIS IS ALL SOUNDING PRETTY GOOD SO FAR. ONTO PAGE 79!
MUCH MUCH LATER
ZZZZzzzz!
AND THAT CONCLUDES CLAUSE 241. WELP, THIS ALL SEEMS PRETTY STANDARD. NOW LETS GET TO THE ACTUAL GAME!
!!!
BEEP BEEP BEEP BEEP
WELL, I GOTTA GO! MY DADS ONLY ALLOW ME THIRTY MINUTES OF VIDEO GAMES PER DAY!
BEEP BEEP
FISH BRAWLER 4
EX ALPHA
MODERN AQUATIC COMBAT
—PRESS START—
END

# "BRACE FOR IT"

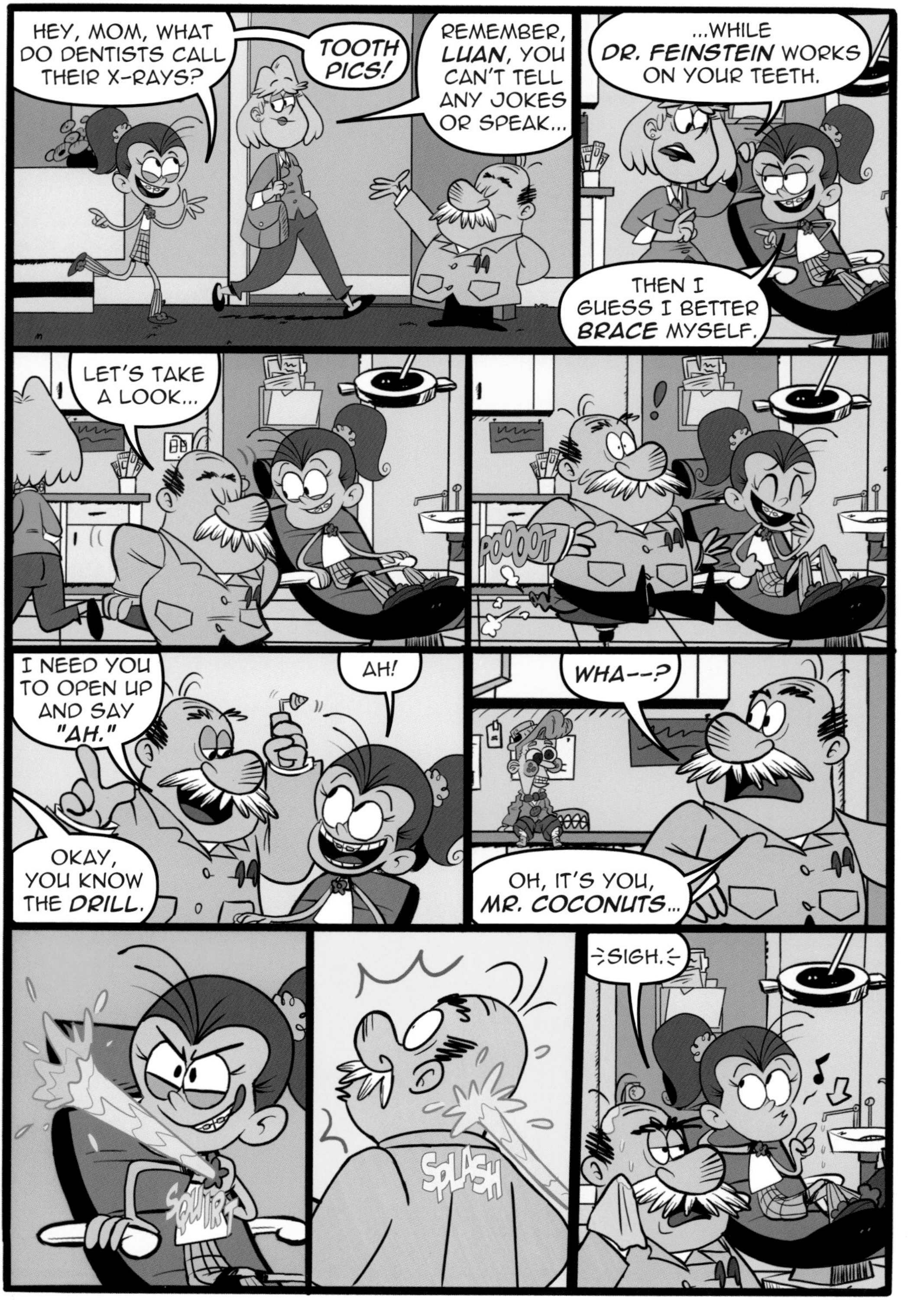

HEY, MOM, WHAT DO DENTISTS CALL THEIR X-RAYS?
TOOTH PICS!
REMEMBER, LUAN, YOU CAN'T TELL ANY JOKES OR SPEAK...
...WHILE DR. FEINSTEIN WORKS ON YOUR TEETH.
THEN I GUESS I BETTER BRACE MYSELF.
LET'S TAKE A LOOK...
POOOOT
I NEED YOU TO OPEN UP AND SAY "AH."
AH!
OKAY, YOU KNOW THE DRILL.
WHA--?
OH, IT'S YOU, MR. COCONUTS...
SQUIRT
SPLASH
SIGH.

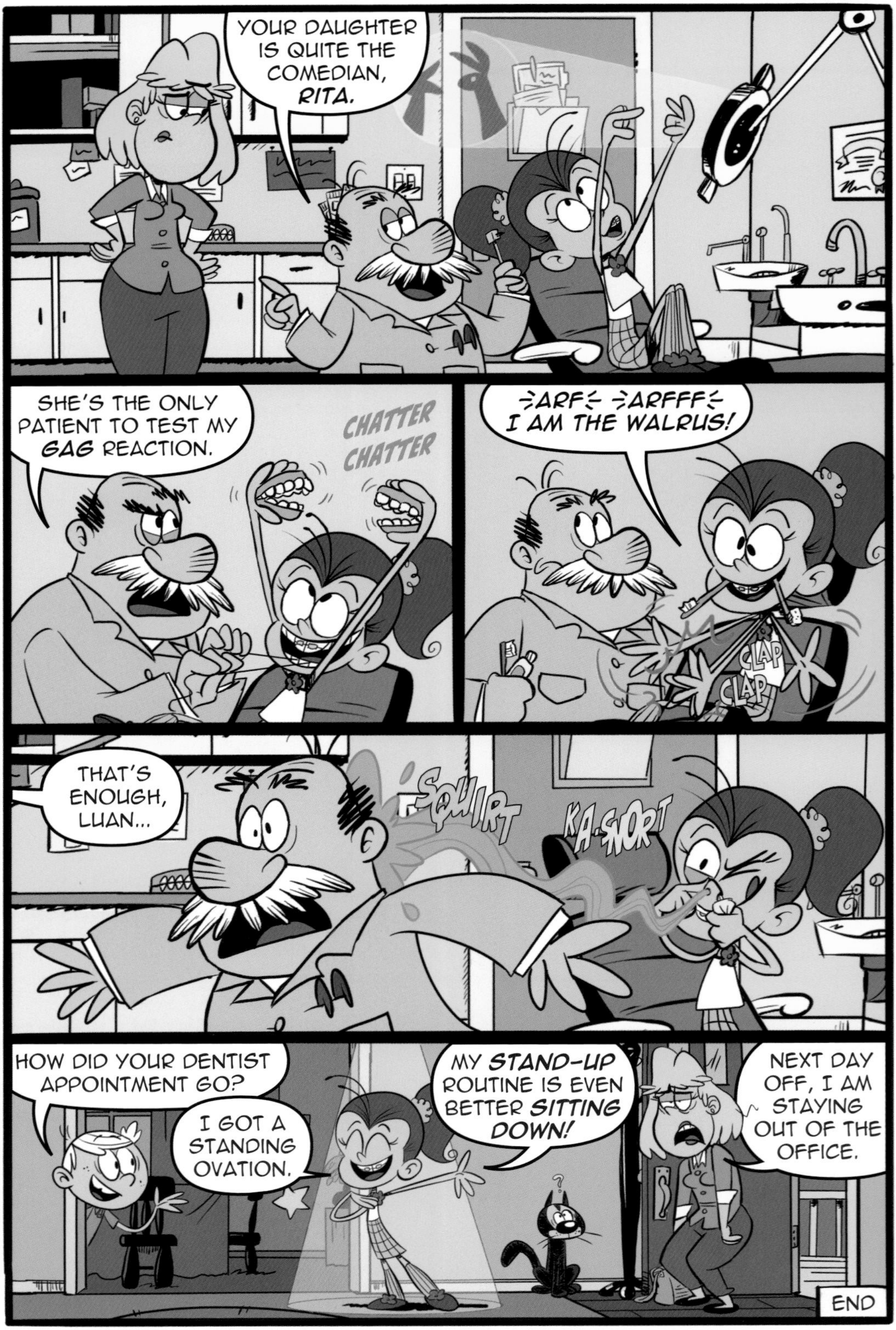
YOUR DAUGHTER IS QUITE THE COMEDIAN, RITA.
SHE'S THE ONLY PATIENT TO TEST MY GAG REACTION.
CHATTER CHATTER
ARF ARFFF I AM THE WALRUS!
CLAP CLAP CLAP
THAT'S ENOUGH, LUAN...
SQUIRT
KA-SNORT
HOW DID YOUR DENTIST APPOINTMENT GO?
I GOT A STANDING OVATION.
MY STAND-UP ROUTINE IS EVEN BETTER SITTING DOWN!
NEXT DAY OFF, I AM STAYING OUT OF THE OFFICE.
END

# "CANDY HUNTING AT HUNTINGTON MANOR"

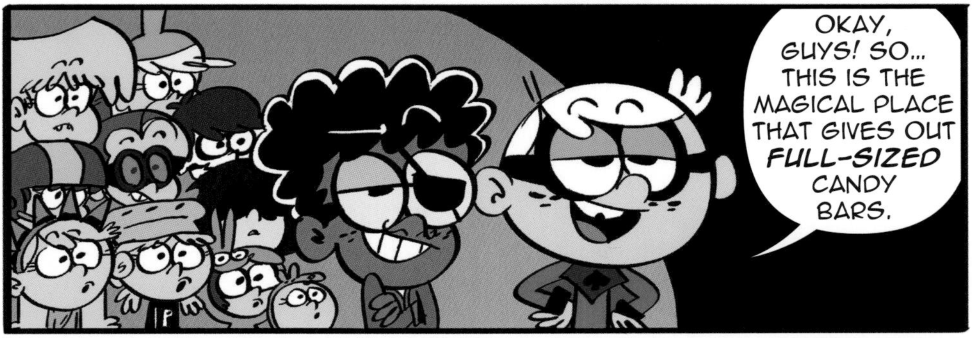
OKAY, GUYS! SO... THIS IS THE MAGICAL PLACE THAT GIVES OUT *FULL-SIZED* CANDY BARS.

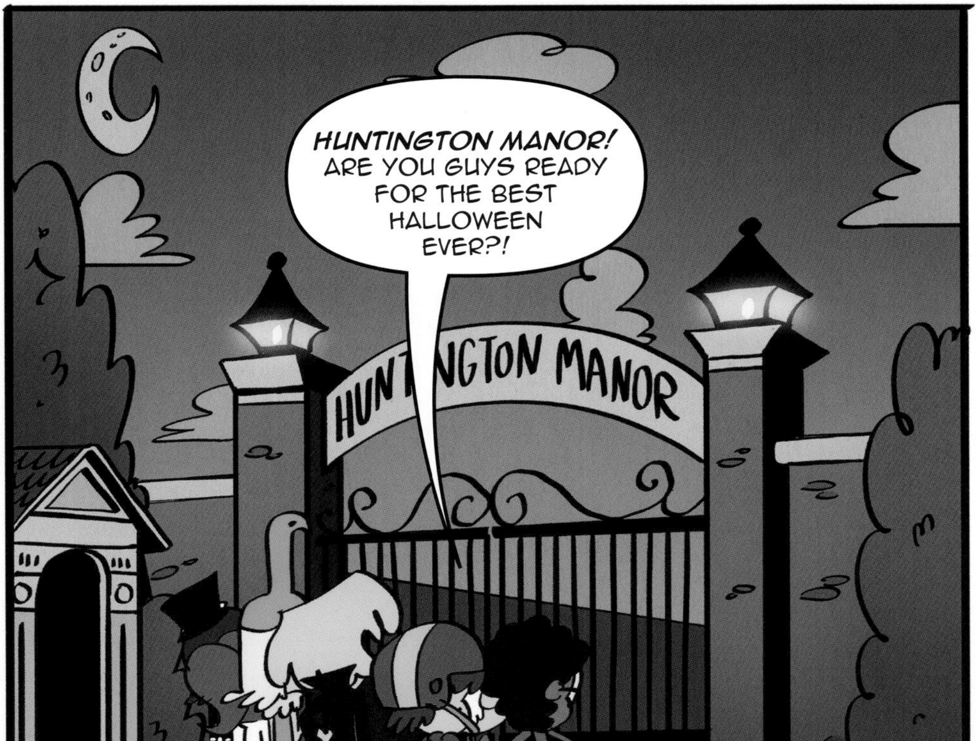
*HUNTINGTON MANOR!* ARE YOU GUYS READY FOR THE BEST HALLOWEEN EVER?!
HUN NGTON MANOR

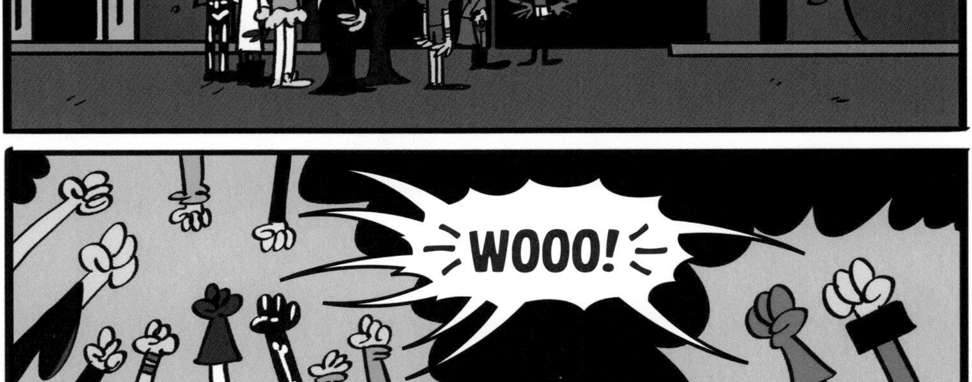
WOOO!

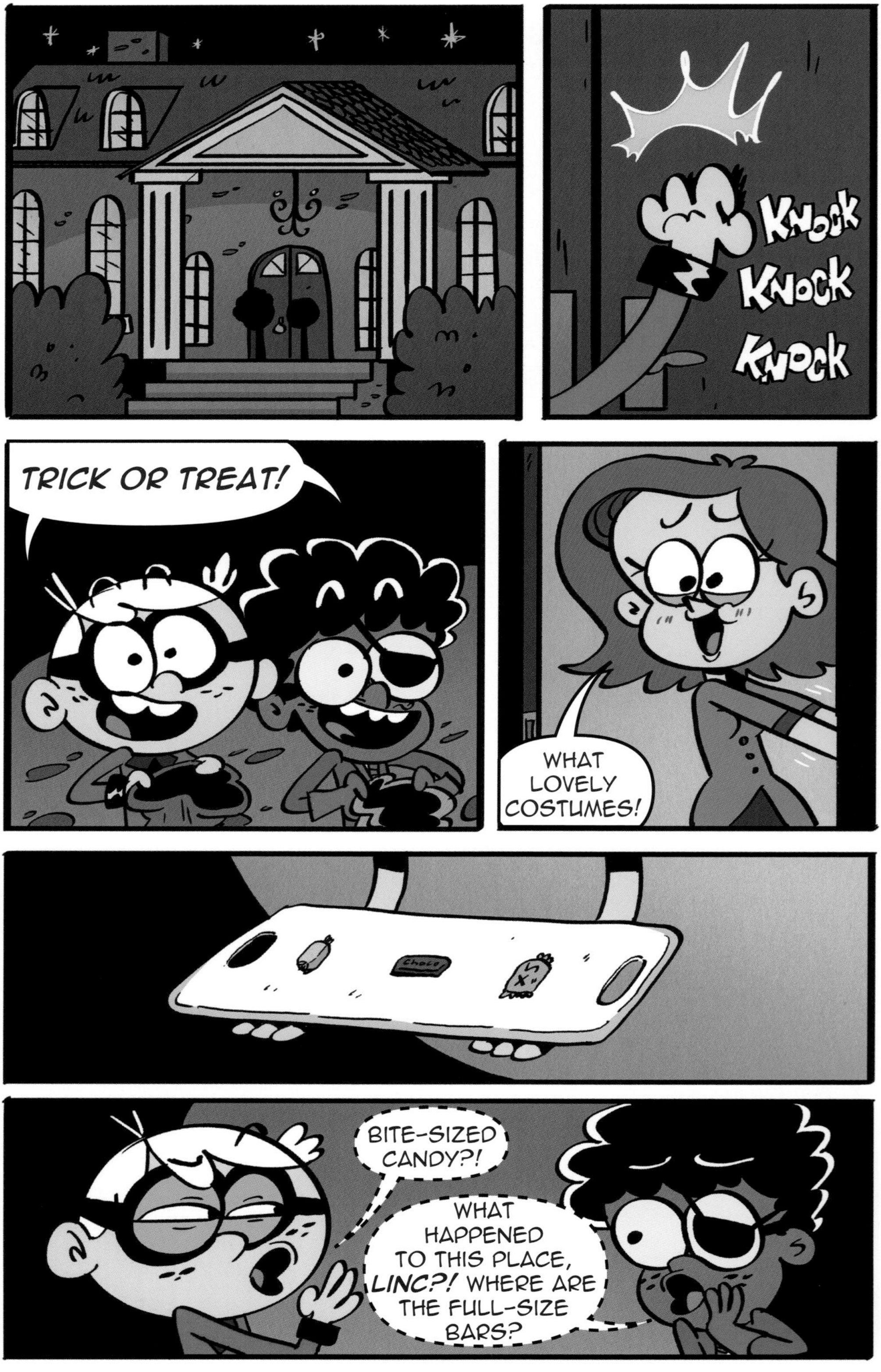
KNOCK
KNOCK
KNOCK
TRICK OR TREAT!
WHAT LOVELY COSTUMES!
BITE-SIZED CANDY?!
WHAT HAPPENED TO THIS PLACE, *LINC?!* WHERE ARE THE FULL-SIZE BARS?

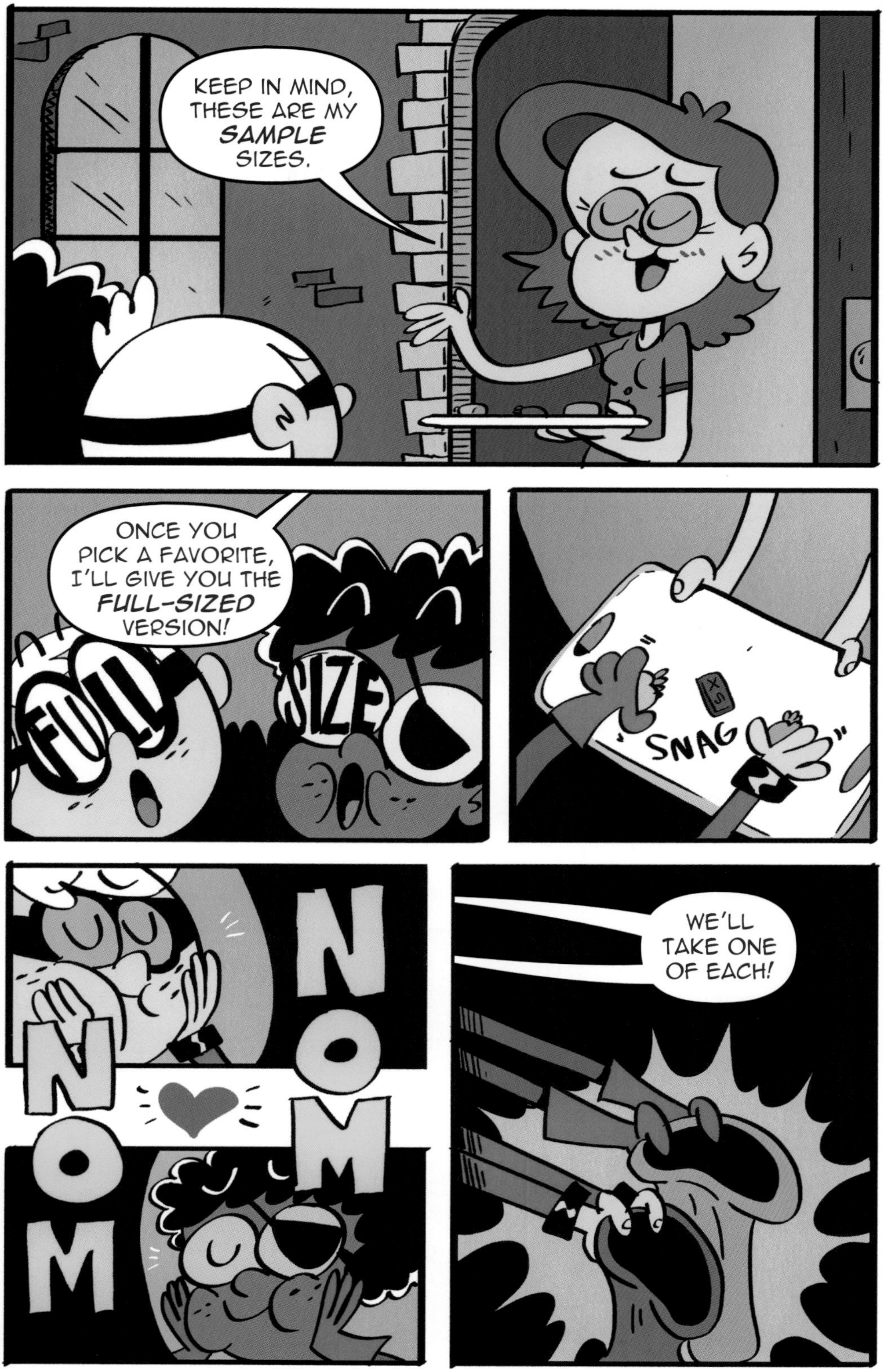
KEEP IN MIND, THESE ARE MY SAMPLE SIZES.
ONCE YOU PICK A FAVORITE, I'LL GIVE YOU THE FULL-SIZED VERSION!
FULL
SIZE
XS
SNAG
NOM
NOM
WE'LL TAKE ONE OF EACH!

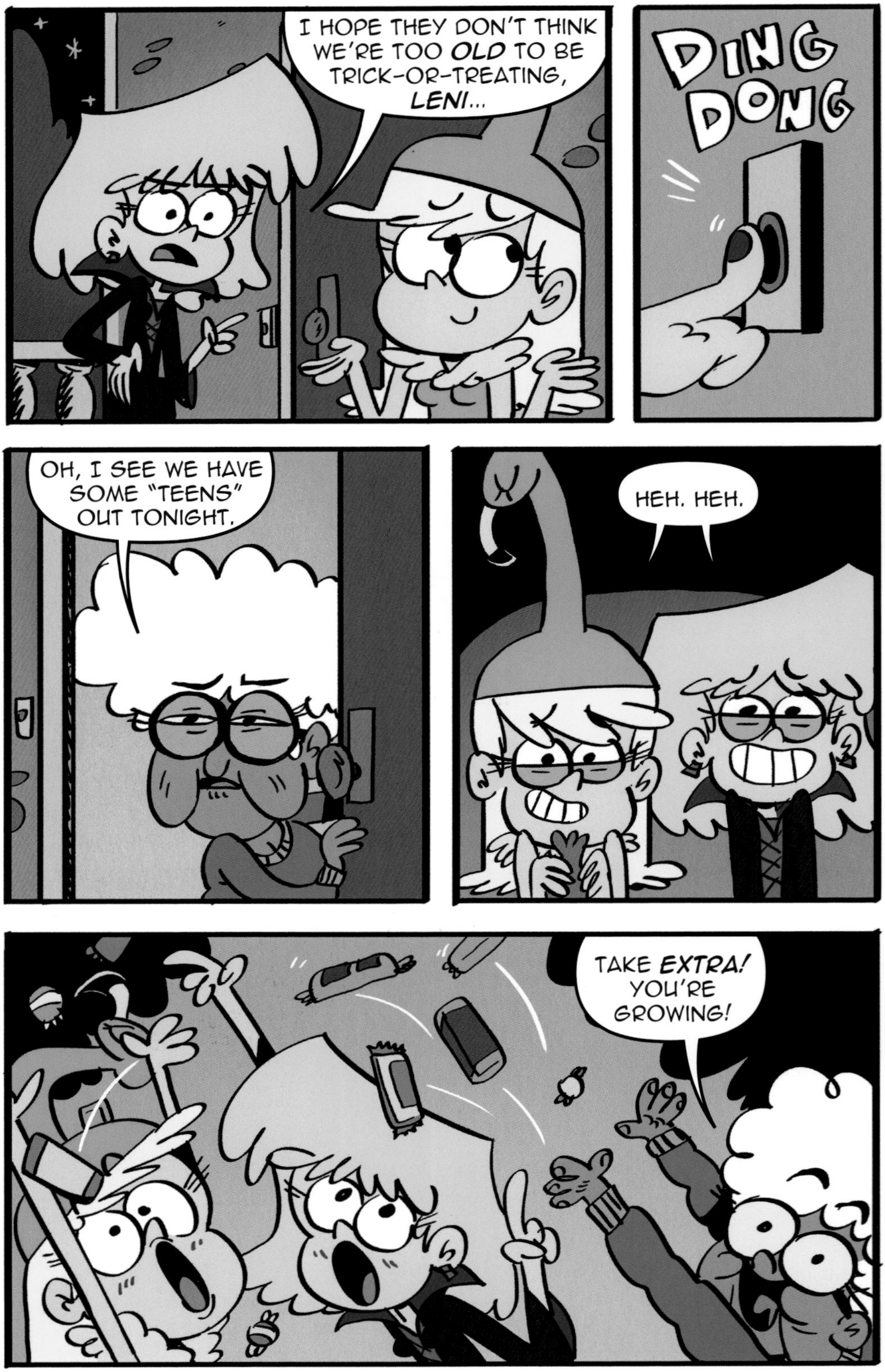
I HOPE THEY DON'T THINK WE'RE TOO ***OLD*** TO BE TRICK-OR-TREATING, ***LENI***...
DING DONG
OH, I SEE WE HAVE SOME "TEENS" OUT TONIGHT.
HEH. HEH.
TAKE ***EXTRA!*** YOU'RE GROWING!

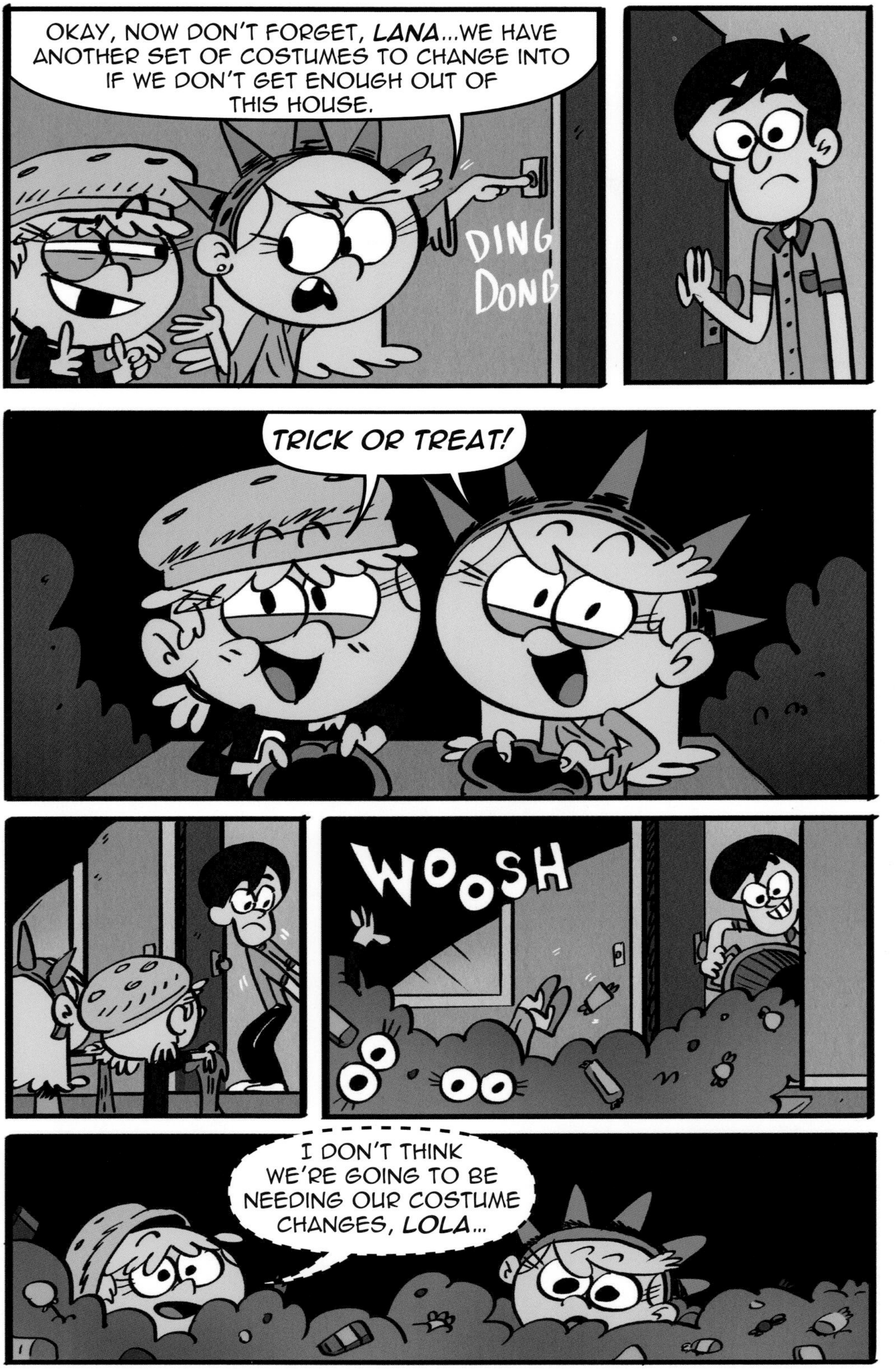
OKAY, NOW DON'T FORGET, LANA...WE HAVE ANOTHER SET OF COSTUMES TO CHANGE INTO IF WE DON'T GET ENOUGH OUT OF THIS HOUSE.
DING DONG
TRICK OR TREAT!
WOOSH
I DON'T THINK WE'RE GOING TO BE NEEDING OUR COSTUME CHANGES, LOLA...

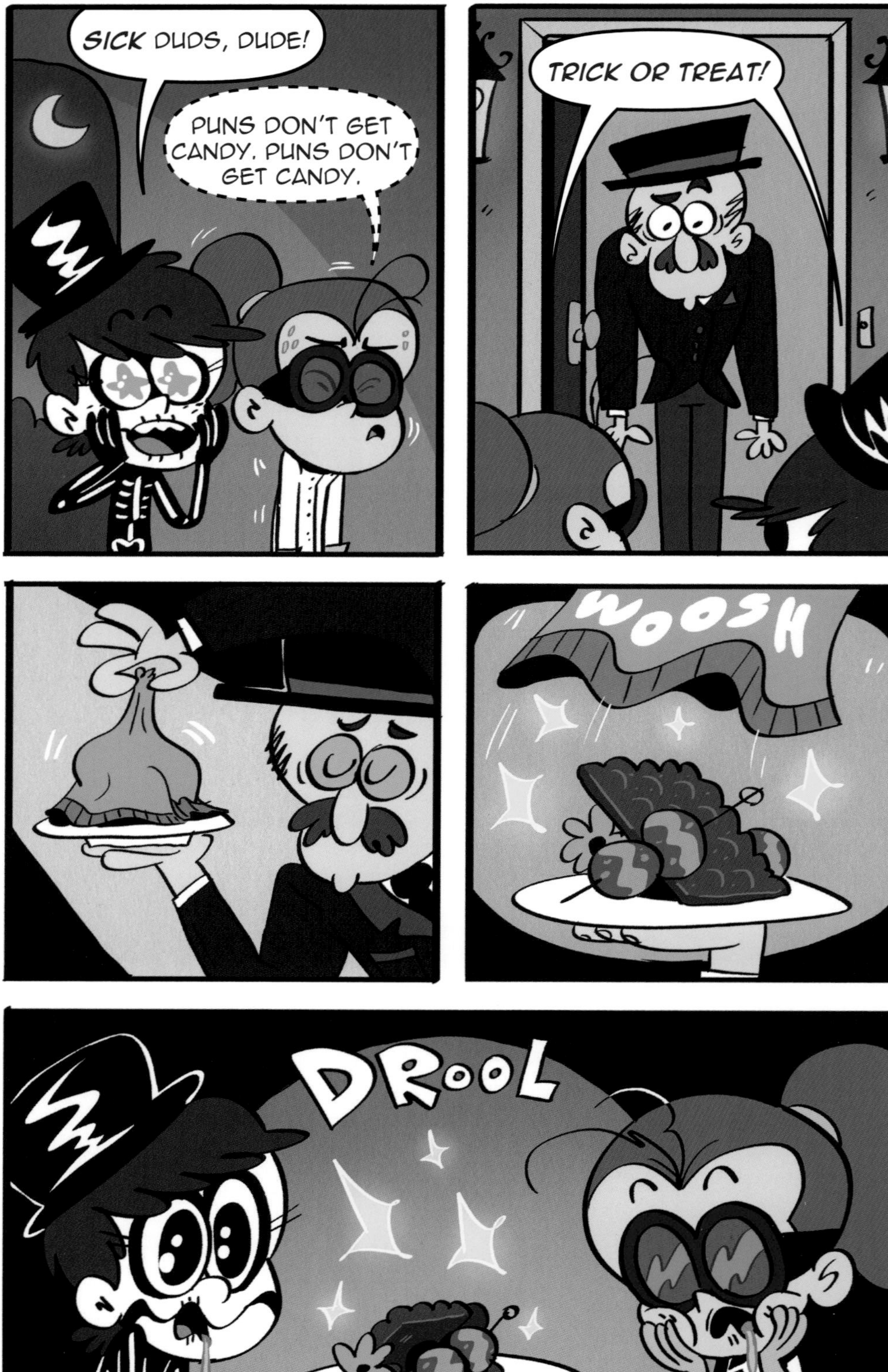
SICK DUDS, DUDE!
PUNS DON'T GET CANDY. PUNS DON'T GET CANDY.
TRICK OR TREAT!
WOOSH
DROOL

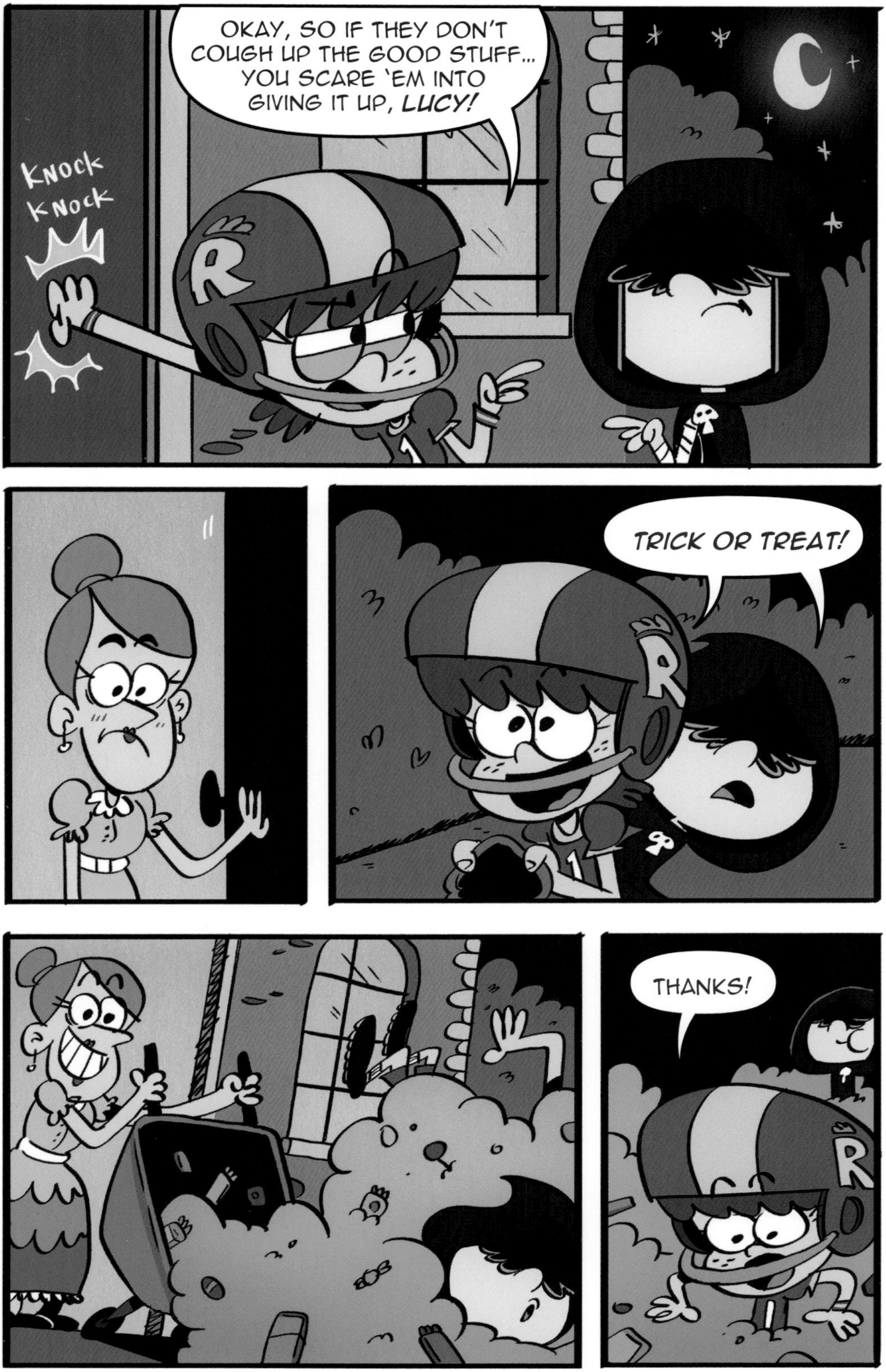
KNOCK KNOCK
OKAY, SO IF THEY DON'T COUGH UP THE GOOD STUFF... YOU SCARE 'EM INTO GIVING IT UP, *LUCY!*
*TRICK OR TREAT!*
THANKS!

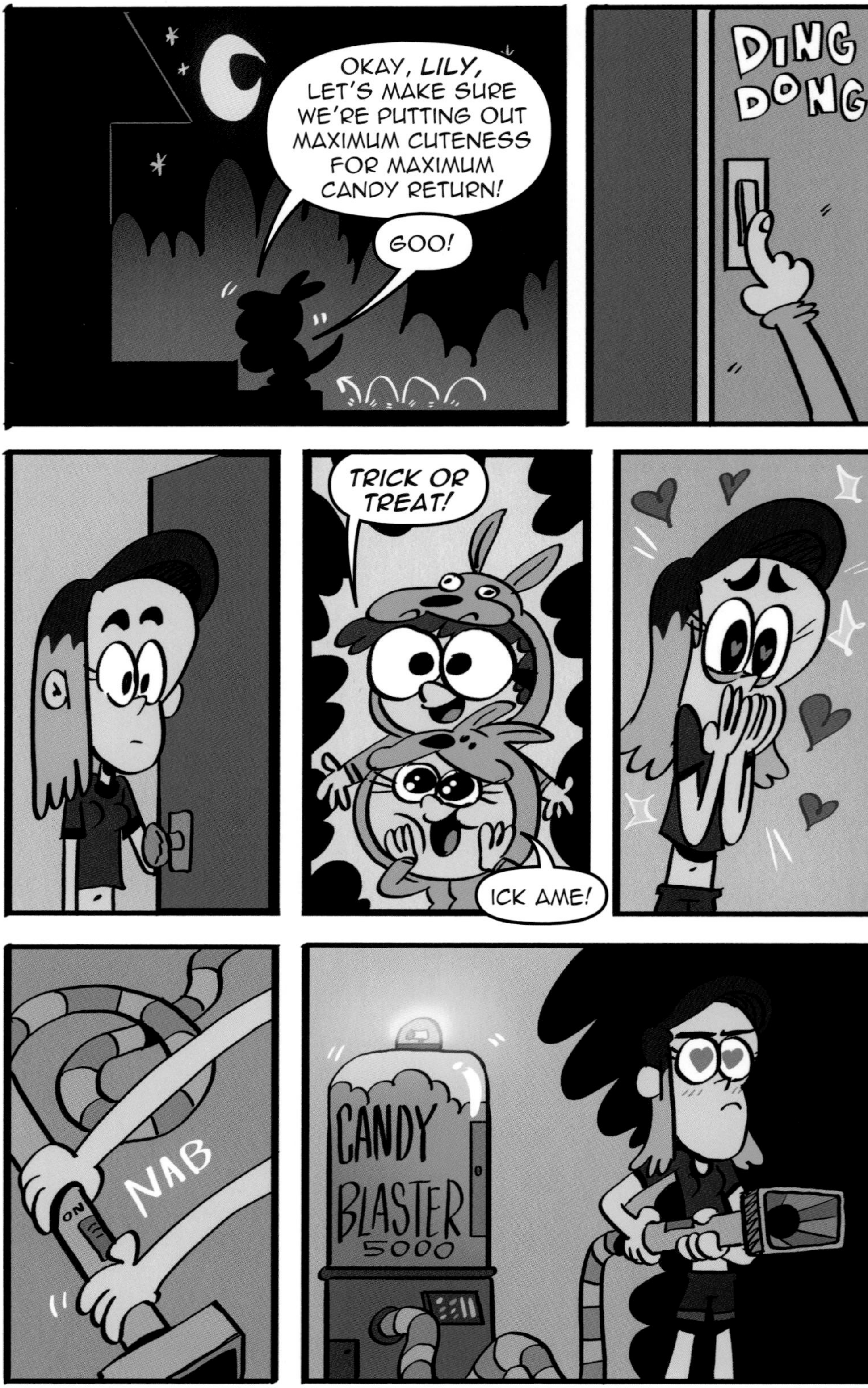
OKAY, LILY, LET'S MAKE SURE WE'RE PUTTING OUT MAXIMUM CUTENESS FOR MAXIMUM CANDY RETURN!
GOO!
DING DONG
TRICK OR TREAT!
ICK AME!
NAB
ON
CANDY BLASTER 5000

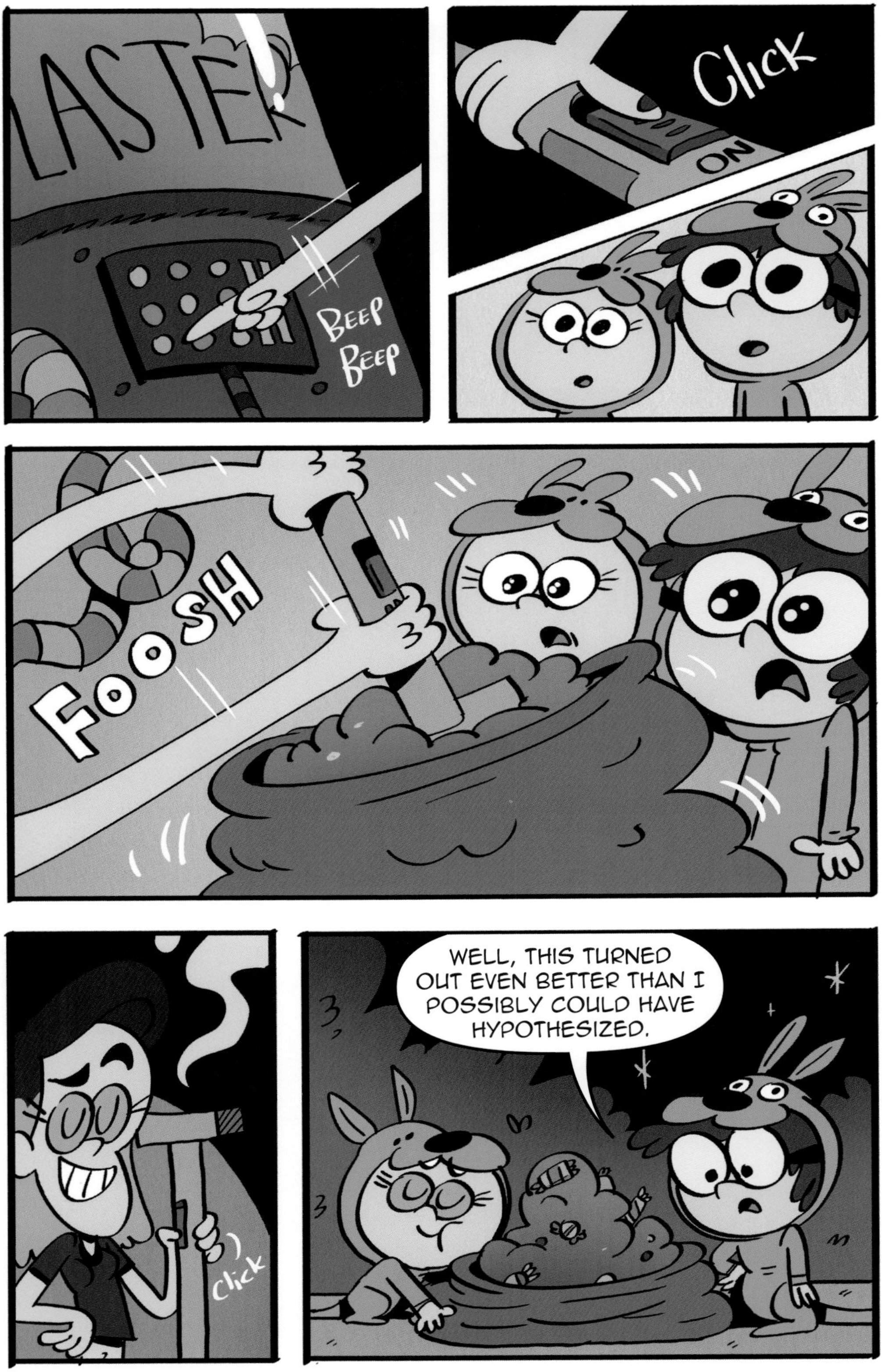

BEEP
BEEP
CLICK
ON
FOOSH
CLICK
WELL, THIS TURNED OUT EVEN BETTER THAN I POSSIBLY COULD HAVE HYPOTHESIZED.

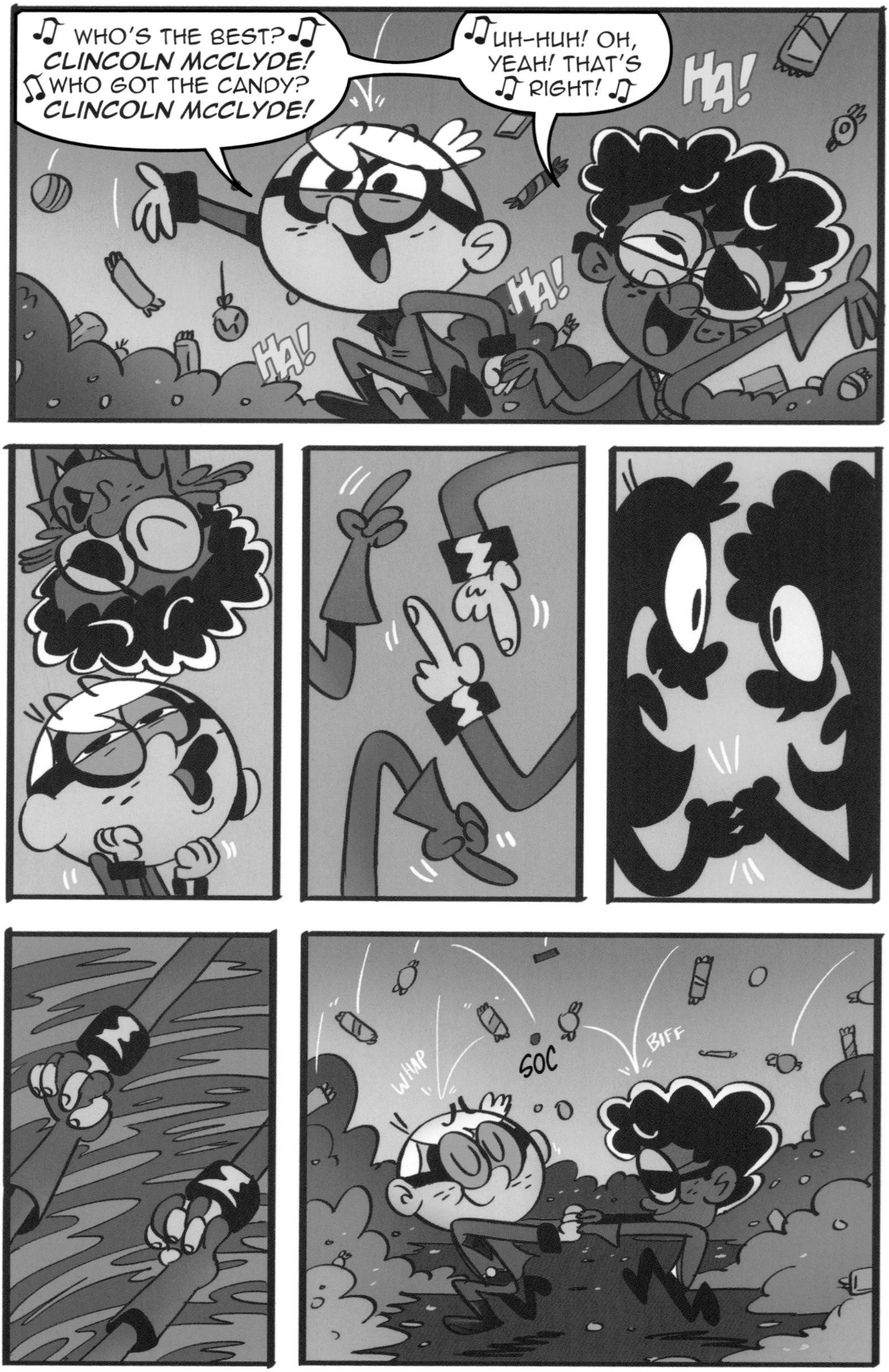
♫ WHO'S THE BEST? ♫ CLINCOLN McCLYDE! ♫ WHO GOT THE CANDY? CLINCOLN McCLYDE!
♫ UH-HUH! OH, YEAH! THAT'S ♫ RIGHT! ♫
HA!
HA!
HA!
WHAP
SOC
BIFF

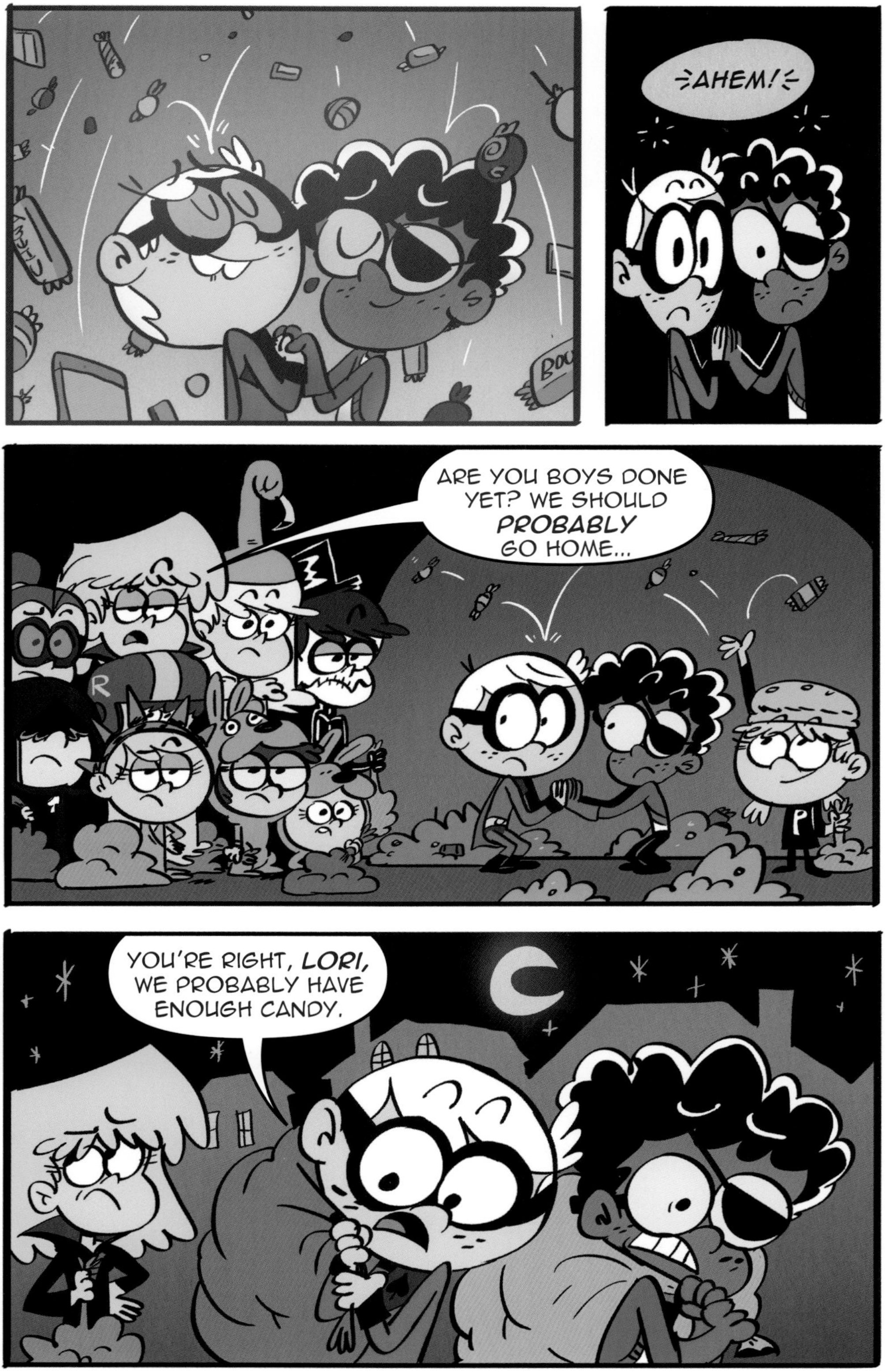
AHEM!
ARE YOU BOYS DONE YET? WE SHOULD PROBABLY GO HOME...
YOU'RE RIGHT, LORI, WE PROBABLY HAVE ENOUGH CANDY.

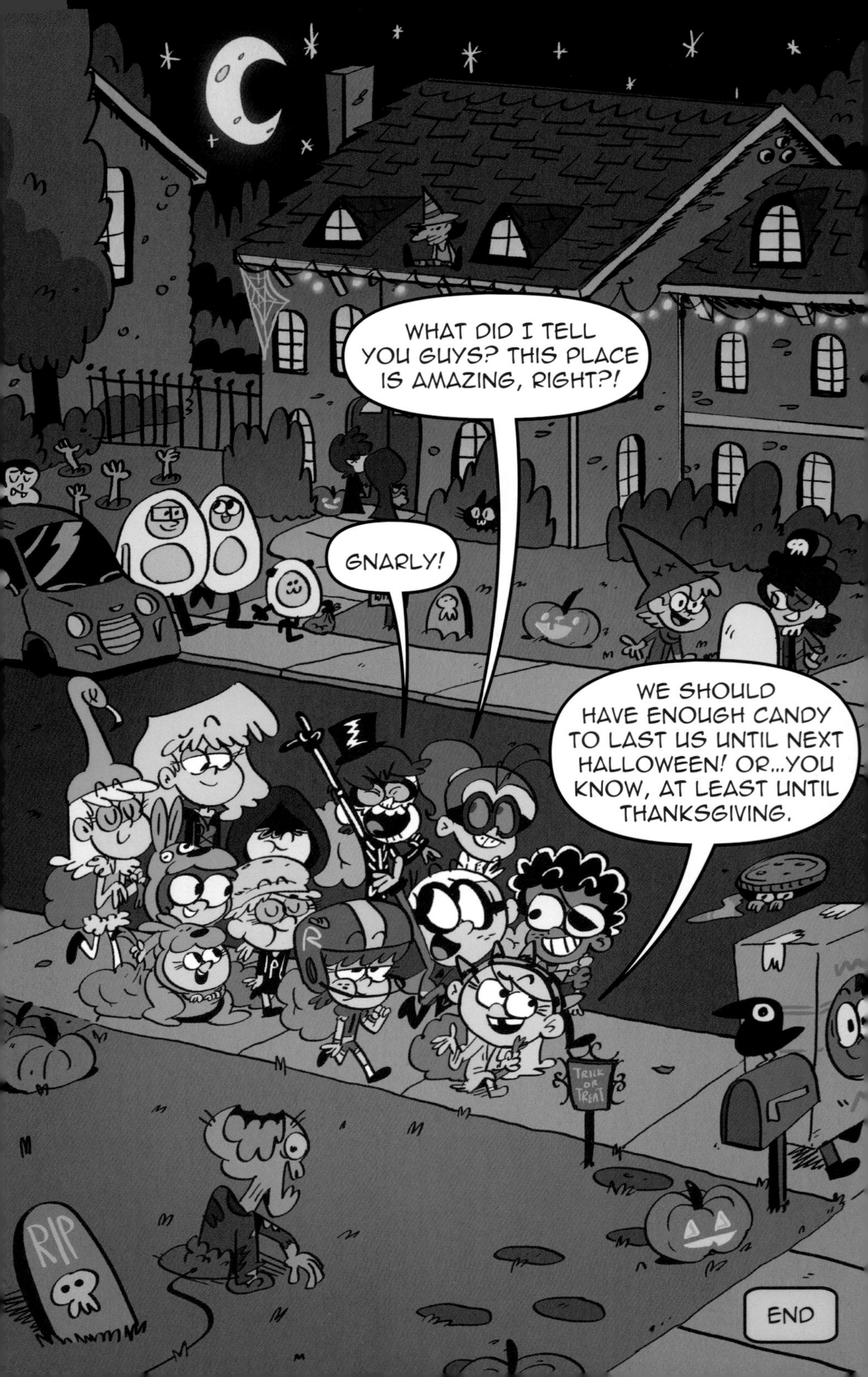
WHAT DID I TELL YOU GUYS? THIS PLACE IS AMAZING, RIGHT?!
GNARLY!
WE SHOULD HAVE ENOUGH CANDY TO LAST US UNTIL NEXT HALLOWEEN! OR...YOU KNOW, AT LEAST UNTIL THANKSGIVING.
TRICK OR TREAT
RIP
END

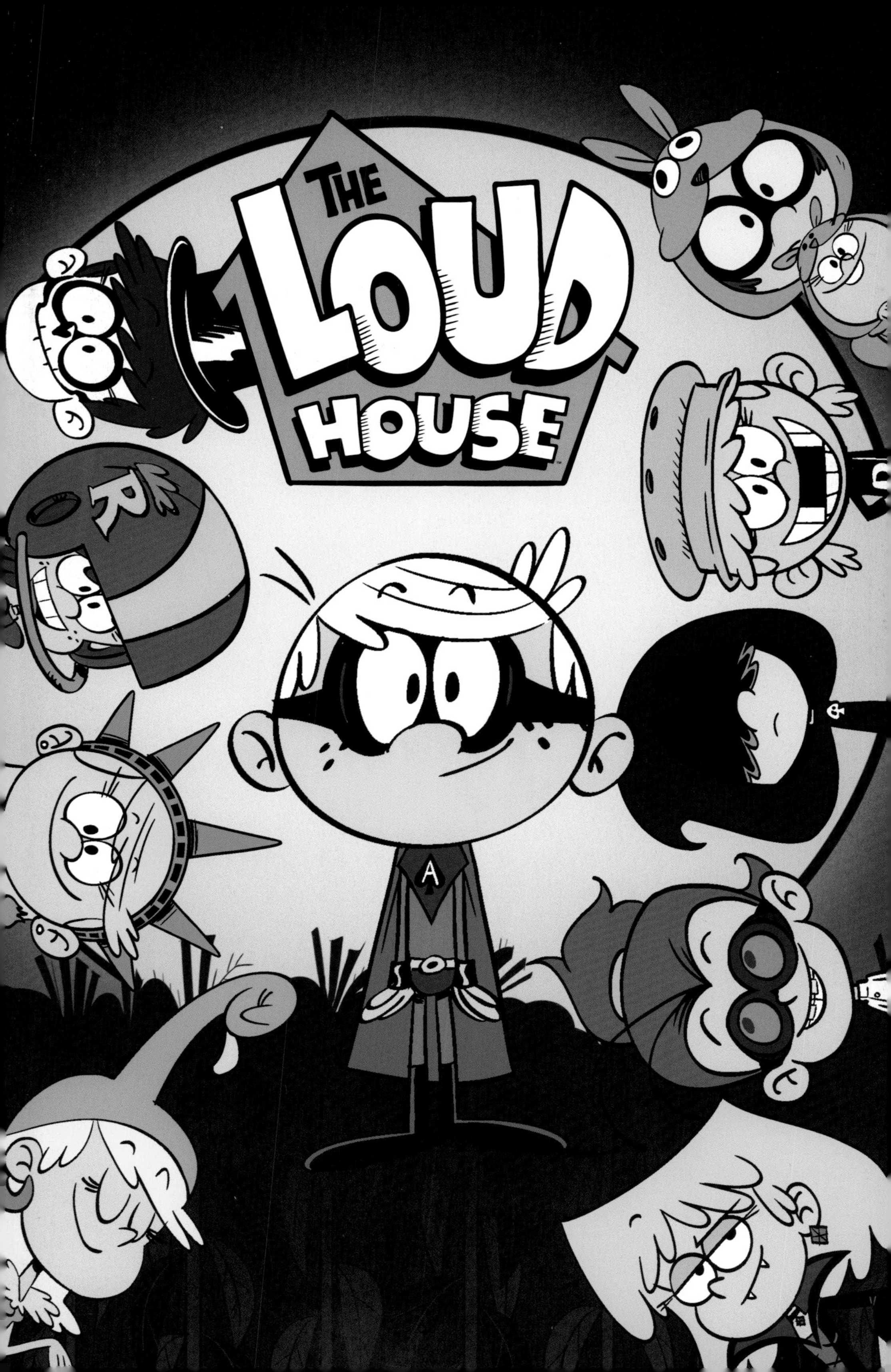
THE LOUD HOUSE

# WATCH OUT FOR PAPERCUTZ™

Welcome to the twinsiest tome yet—the tenth THE LOUD HOUSE graphic novel "The Many Faces of Lincoln Loud," from Papercutz, those multiple personalities dedicated to publishing great graphic novels for all ages. I'm Jim Salicrup, Editor-in-Chief and one of the two Gemini Papercutz business partners. Gemini is the zodiac sign of the Twins, and while Papercutz publisher Terry Nantier and I aren't actual twins, we were born four days apart, but we're about as different from each other as the twin Loud sisters. While you'll find a great Lola & Lana adventure in these pages, mostly we're celebrating all the other guises that Lincoln Loud takes on. From Ace Savvy to Clincoln McCloud, our man Linc takes role-playing to new heights!

You know, once when I was a kid I had a dual identity without even realizing it! A friend's mother thought I was two different people—once when I hadn't had a haircut for a while (I had long curly black hair back then) and then after I got a haircut (she liked the short-haired me best). Do you have a tale of two identities?.

In various other Papercutz graphic novels, dual identities are not all that uncommon. In THE MYTHICS #1 "Heroes Reborn," for example, we meet three kids from around the world who soon become super-powered incarnations of old powerful beings. Please, allow me to introduce them…

The god of lightning, Raijin, instills his powers in Yuko, a Japanese schoolgirl in a rock band. Yuko must learn to wield her newfound electrical powers to defeat Fuijin, the evil god of wind, before he destroys all of Japan.

Meanwhile, in Egypt, young Amir, a recently orphaned boy taking over his father's successful company and landholdings, encounters Horus, the Sun and Moon god. Horus and Amir must stop evil, in the form of Seth, from reanimating all the dead mummies and taking over the world.

Lastly, a young opera hopeful, Abigail, must face a blizzard freezing all of Germany orchestrated by Loki, the evil god of mischief. Under the guidance of Freyja, the Norse god of beauty, Abigail must find her voice and her mythic weapon to stop evil in its tracks.

You can meet all three in THE MYTHICS #1, available now wherever you get your graphic novels.

Cazenove • William

THE SUPER SISTERS

PAPERCUTZ

While the kids from THE MYTHICS literally turn into different beings, over in THE SISTERS, Maureen and Wendy often imagine themselves as having super-powers and battling all kinds of villains and monsters. In fact, that part of the series proved to be so popular, there's an entire SUPER SISTERS graphic novel devoted to new, longer versions of those imaginary adventures. It too, is available now at your favorite booksellers and libraries. And that's exactly where you'll soon find THE LOUD HOUSE #11, featuring more fun with Lincoln, his ten sisters, and all their friends and families. We're sure you won't want to miss it!

Thanks,

JIM

## STAY IN TOUCH!

EMAIL: salicrup@papercutz.com
WEB: papercutz.com
TWITTER: @papercutzgn
INSTAGRAM: @papercutzgn
FACEBOOK: PAPERCUTZGRAPHICNOVELS
FANMAIL: Papercutz, 160 Broadway, Suite 700, East Wing, New York, NY 10038

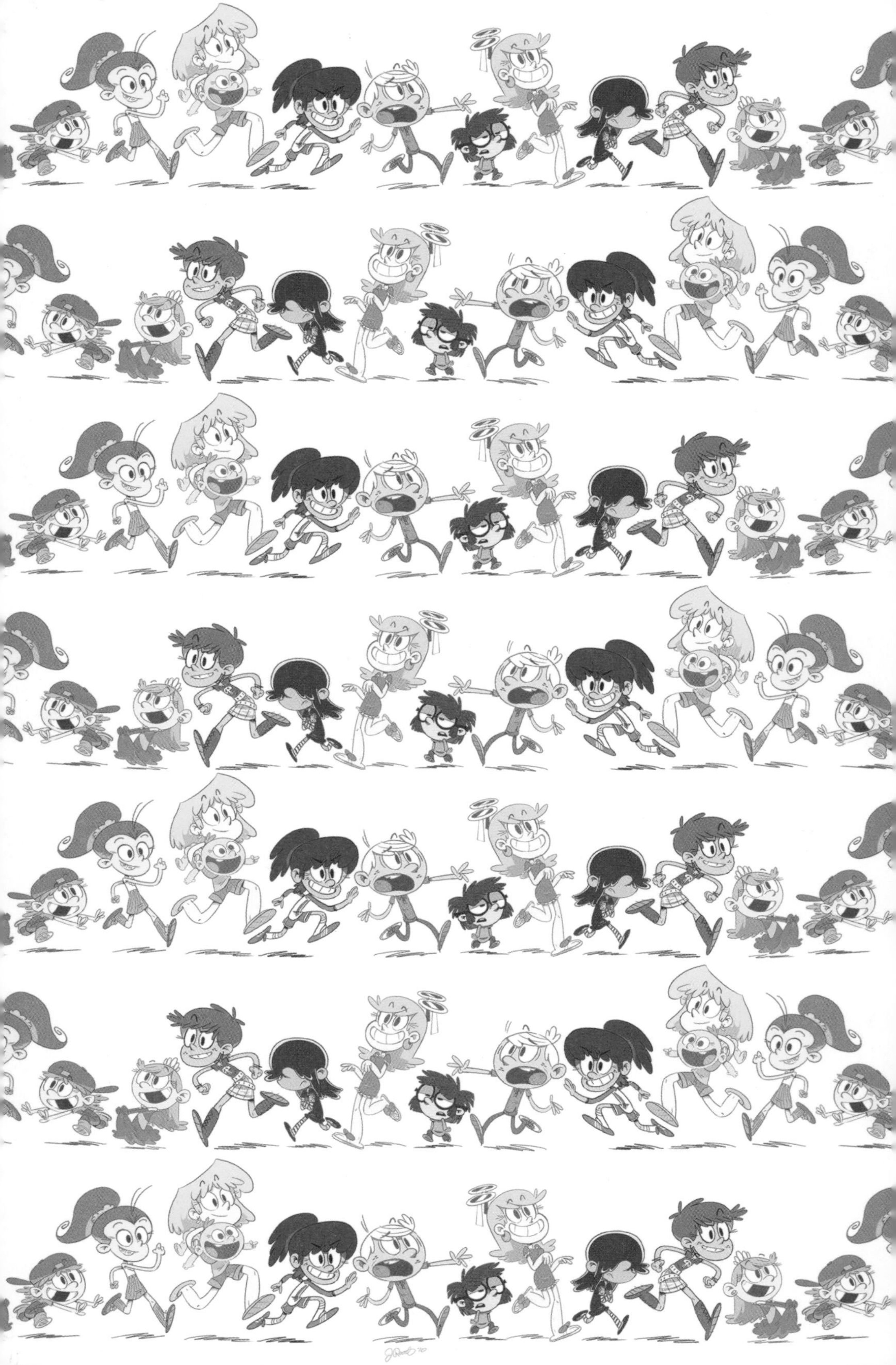